I0831375

PRAISE FOR BESTGHOST

"For me, it was magnificently spooky and the ending gave me a visceral reaction I won't soon forget. Whenever I close my eyes it's as if I'm still in that room..." **-Ash, FANFIADDICT.com**

"As someone who religiously binge watched all of Buzzfeed Unsolved: Supernatural, this 'ghost hunting gone wrong' story gave me everything I didn't know I needed from a horror short story." **-Esmay, BEFOREWE GOBLOG.com**

"This is such a delightfully spooky treat that's perfect for the fall! The story is funny, but also spooky, and gave me chills at parts!" **-Helen Power, author of THE GHOSTS OF THORWALD PLACE and PHANTOM**

"A quick and spooky read from someone who knows exactly what they're doing. Looking forward to reading more!" **-Mark Towse, author of NANA and CHASING THE DRAGON**

"I read it at midnight and got properly spooked. I am amazed at how much the author is able to achieve with just two guys, their YouTube channel, a haunted mansion, and a pizza delivery" **-Pippin, FANFIADDICT.com**

"Unsettling, nicely constructed and very authentic, it takes everything from old paranormal movies/games and replicates them fantastically" **-EJ Doble, author of THE FANGS OF WAR and THE CRESCENT MOON**

C. J. DALEY

TALES FROM CEMETERY

TALES FROM CEMETERY

A Short Story Collection

By C. J. Daley

Cover art by Matt Seff Barnes
BestGhost Books Logo created by Miblart
Title page images from Stock Photos & Canva
No Generative AI has been used in the making of this collection
Edited by Ed Crocker
BestGhost edited by Amber Herbert / Proofread by Ed Crocker
First Edition

To Em, III, and Clair-o
I will make you proud

Two of you better not read this until you are way older...

CONTENT WARNING

Cursing, bullying, confinement, grief, thoughts of suicide, death, violence, gun violence, kidnapping, blood and gore, murder

INTRODUCTION

When I had the original idea for the town of Cemetery, I had never written anything to completion before. I had what I thought was a solid idea, but no clue as to what level it would reach. My general beginning was that it would be a novella with accompanying horror short stories, released into a single collection (i.e., *Cemetery AND Other Stories*...or something like it). When *Welcome to Cemetery* eventually grew into an entire novel, all I knew for sure was that I didn't want to scrap all the short story ideas. My original Cemetery idea was much more along of the lines of straight horror, but as the plot began to take shape, it became more of the crime thriller/horror that it is today. I was relatively new to horror when writing these, so this was much more about playing in the sandbox of what already was, as opposed to reinventing the wheel. So a lot of these short stories are straight horror. Several of them are more in the supernatural world or sillier than Cemetery's actual grounded universe, but I thought they'd be fun to share anyway.

The eleventh story, the extra, "Off With Their Sleds," is a direct sequel to *Welcome to Cemetery*, and as such, contains spoilers if you've not read the novel. That's why it's the eleventh story, a bonus if you will. I just really wanted to write a Christmas mystery.

Perhaps you even caught a few of the stories' easter eggs in the novel? Maybe you'll go back and check someday...

C. J. Daley

2023–25

CONTENTS

WELCOME TO CEMETERY

(Excerpt from Welcome to Cemetery)

The town of Cemetery, New York sat damn-near invisibly among the other villages of the Hudson River Valley. It's not that it was hard to find, or out of the way. Nor was it that hidden—practically only an hour outside New York City. Rather, it was just typically forgotten. Most of the townsfolk thought that the name was funny or silly originally, but with the passing of time, they started to think that it was part of the reason it was overlooked—as if people couldn't get past the fact that the name was of an entire town and not a place. "What was the name of that town again?" visitors might ask each other while passing through. "I don't remember, I think I only saw a sign for the cemetery."

The town itself had a single long road that ran the entire length of it called Route 17. This was from the time long forgotten when a route or highway could be labeled for a single two-lane road. The townsfolk just referred to it as Main Street. However, any single turn off the main street was practically, and immediately, back road. A neighbor might be several turns away, but only a short drive or walk away.

Not overpopulated, streets were filled with trees. American beech, sugar maples, yellow birch, and great swaths of pine trees stretched way high into the sky. Cemetery wasn't known for any single trade, but more often than not, truck advertisements and tee shirts in supermarket lines boasting employment with *Cemetery Town & Lumber* could be seen. Some might say the town and the surrounding area were beautiful; it just didn't stand out above the rest.

Demographically, Cemetery was of an average size, in an average area, with average workers, townsfolk, and children; an average climate; and even an average unemployment rate. The only thing about Cemetery that wasn't average, was the number of crimes that went unsolved and unpunished.

Now it wasn't that the police force was too small, too negligent, too unproven. It was simply that they were inundated with a mysterious, arguably devilish level of disappearances and deaths, and insufficient evidence to solve them. Even with the most experienced wracking their brains for a solution, a lead, or a single shred of evidence, nothing was found, and nothing was solved. Over the years, many of the retirees from the police department became true crime enthusiasts, taking to continued researching and speculation over crimes long unsolved in their newly found free time. One group that had gotten a semi-substantial following, started calling themselves Closed Case Resurgence. The team worked hard to keep alive the hope on cases long put aside.

Regardless of the way the townsfolk felt about the town, their way of life was often marred with shock and loss, as if a long shadow was cast over the town a long time ago.

Enough time spent somewhere begins to feel like home...

RIGATONI CARL

Nobody Likes the Clown – 1996

Carl Stratton worked his way through the job fair, looking over shoulders and backpacks to see various faces and signs. The booths in straight rows up and down the oversized gymnasium of Cemetery High School packed the room to capacity, the created lanes alarmingly crammed with students and staff alike. The close quarters and heavy traffic made for an odoriferous experience, Carl forced to swallow a laugh at all the cheap cologne and bodily odor crowding the air like a pubescent smog.

A booth for *Cemetery Town & Lumber* stood out like a sore thumb; only those of the truly desperate variety would sign up for years of wood-chipped clothes and splinters. Then again, he had passed the booth for the Cemetery Police Department, the inexplicable fact that there was a line showing just how impressionable the youths truly were. One of the officers stared a second longer than he would have liked, but then he was gone.

Carl's smile widened.

He didn't have a job to offer, but these things were always so packed that the schools never noticed one more adult. If they happened to ask, he'd say he was making the rounds for his stall. They never asked.

Carl licked his lips, biting the lower one hard and trying his damnedest to keep in a giggle. These things were simply too fun. He loved the idea of blending in, completely unseen, his ability to weave among the kids without consequence the funniest part. He could interact, touch, or take any one of them, and no one would stop him or even notice.

Lucky for them, was the fact that these near-adults were getting too old for that. Too old for *Rigatoni* more specifically. But after waking lonely yet again, there was nothing stopping him.

See, Carl was a part-time clown. Not a very successful one, but that was beside the point. His use of the term "part-time" was even a stretch, but the work he did bring in was enough to keep him going, to satiate him.

Rigatoni Carl, as he had dubbed himself, was the proudly successful clown of over twenty parties. Months later, the attendees of these parties found themselves the victims of playground kidnappings, assaults, and vicious killings. No one knew that for sure, though. They were simply referred to as *abductions* or *missing children* in all of the news clippings Carl would hoard and tack to his bedroom walls. And wasn't the idea of kids on milk cartoons so very funny?

"*Have you seen poor Jimmy Costa?*" Carl almost said out loud as he scooted his way between another group of kids. His cackle followed, as he imagined children idly looking at the picture on the milk as they ate their sugary, teeth-rotting cereal. He covered his mouth, as if he could reverse the release, ducking his chin to his chest and looking to the floor. The kids that overheard gave him a wide berth after that, but Carl didn't care.

Mere moments from then he'd be invisible again.

For someone who loved being invisible at public events, it always struck Carl as odd that his therapist constantly harped on about the fact that he truly needed to be *seen*, something or other about his parents' mistreatment leading to a loss of identity. As if having someone to understand him would make him whole. As if having a significant other would stave off the urges, the calling. If only they knew his real day job. You couldn't practice vivisection on a girlfriend and hope that they'd stay. At least not of their own accord. Unless his therapist had known something? Did she perhaps mean he should let someone in on his secret, to share the experience? A partner in his literal crimes? A two-clown operation perhaps? Carl wondered if she had meant herself.

Yes, Carl was probably broken. He saw the therapist for a reason of course, but wasn't this just a load of fun?

"Hi, what's your name?" one of the near-adults asked, drawing him from his musings.

"I'm Rig—I'm Carl...just Carl," he replied with a heavy stutter, running a palm over his buzzed head. He kept his hair short, all the easier to slip into his clown clothes. Carl's face had a crooked nose, not long but decidedly *bent*. His lips, still showing a slight reddish rouge, turned up in a smile.

"Well, hi, Just-Carl," the student said. "What are you hiring for?"

Free lobotomies? Carl thought, *Free amputations*? He instead said, "Oh, I'm so sorry sonny, we've filled our roster with committed interns already! Better luck next time."

Carl giggled, ruffled the student's hair, and walked away without another look.

Carl had been giggling more and more lately, the blend between Carl and Rigatoni becoming increasingly tenuous. As the time between his little parties grew wider, Rigatoni fought his way to the surface harder. *It's time for fun again!*

That was closer than Carl would have liked. Where the hell did that kid even come from? This was, of course, another thing his therapist often pointed out. Carl's habitual need to fantasize and wander while in a public space. The doc claimed it was a way for him to detach, rather than put himself out there, the last people to truly see him having been his parents, and well, that hadn't been so good for Carl, had it? And when your initial instinct is to look for a handy utensil to stab the person in front of you, it's probably best to keep that fantasy to yourself. That seemed obvious enough, if only he could have told her.

As Carl did a final pass, he noticed a group of boys shooting hoops on one of those arcade things. He licked his lips, watching how their muscles moved in their arms with each consecutive shot, wondering what it would be like to saw through them. It was hard for him not to look. The way the muscles stretched and pulled. The strength and location of each. How they would look as they were cut apart, the terror he would inflict as muscle was shaved back from the shoulder joint. He smiled widely when he realized he had been staring, another group of kids beginning to eye him suspiciously. *Goddamn stranger danger campaigns.*

He ignored them, and as one of them broke off from the rest, heading toward the hanging "restrooms" sign, Carl decided to follow. Against his better judgement maybe, but what the hell, he hadn't done anything. Not yet.

Outside the bathroom Carl paused. He stooped to take a long drink from the water fountain, noticing the layered grime that had calcified around the mouthpiece, but not minding. Steeling himself as well as giving the kid time so as not to barge in right behind him.

Carl swung the bathroom door open on silent hinges. The boy didn't even glance up as he walked past him. Another look reminded him again that this was more of an adult, a near-adult, than a boy. However, he was all-in already. No point in denying it.

Carl pushed open the stall door next to the boy. He shut and locked it behind him and approached the wall of the stall, placing his head against the plastic and listening to the boy urinate on the other side. As he listened, as he imagined him right on the other side, his breathing hitched and became heavy. Unable to stop himself, he forced himself against the wall of the stall, his entire torso pressing into the scratched and chipped plastic, the toilet paper rack pressing harshly into his crotch. He breathed harder.

A harsh cutoff to the boy's peeing caused Carl to groan involuntarily.

"I can see your feet from under the stall. What the fuck are you doing, you weirdo?" the student called out, the sound of him zippering himself up hitting Carl like an oversized clown hammer.

Ugh, he really did need to make himself scarce.

BACK THEN

When Carl was eleven, he had come home early from school. He had wet his pants again, and in a disgusted rage, his teacher had kicked him out. It wasn't his fault, but she didn't want to hear it.

He had taken the walk home in shame, passing through the unsavory parts of town without issue. No one wanted to bother a kid with piss dribbling out of his pant leg, the visibly wet and squishing crotch of his jeans giving him a gut-punch of humiliation with each step.

He had entered his house, a nondescript split level hidden from the main road by an overgrown yard and cars propped up on cinderblocks. Carl prayed he could get to his bedroom and change before anyone noticed him. Instead, at the end of the hall, he stood transfixed before the master bedroom.

Carl stared as a man, who was not his father, abusively thrust himself into the woman on the unmade bed. Carl's mother. With each thrust, she made a noise that sounded anything but fun. The man was tall and sweating profusely, the armpits of his wife beater stained a sickly yellow. With each thrust the man seemed to pump himself up further, urging himself to go harder with increased vigor.

All the while Carl stared.

As his mother's eyes finally caught sight of Carl, her body tensed before she rolled over and covered herself. Carl wished he was still at school. Wished he could use the urinals like a normal boy. Could pee in public. Wished he was anywhere but there in that hallway.

Carl's mother stood up off the bed, no longer bothering to cover herself up. She bent down, her exposed and slightly sweaty body coming into horrible focus. He swallowed hard as he stared. She unwound the man's belt from the pants around his ankles, wrapping the worn leather around her hand several times before straightening. As she stepped toward Carl, there was nothing motherly in her eyes.

"How many times I have to tell you to stop interrupting Momma while she pays the rent?"

As the belt repeatedly rained down on Carl, he needed somewhere he could go. Somewhere he could hide.

Or someone who could take the beating for him.

It wasn't until the man, still sweaty and naked from the waist down, entered Carl's room—with or without Momma's consent—that he truly started imagining a means to escape his reality.

1996

Carl stood before the vanity mirror of his bedroom's tiny bathroom. The electric had been shut off again, so he only had a propane lantern for light. He had made himself a ham and cheese sandwich from the fridge. The air inside had still been cold, but the sandwich meat gave off an odd smell. Carl forced another bite into his mouth with a laugh.

They could shut off the lights, the heat, or the water all they liked. What did it matter? Carl didn't care. Wasn't that what made it just a load of fun?

Carl's latest birthday party was worked a little over a month ago. Just long enough for the family to have put him completely out of their minds. Just long enough for him to have mapped out their property, household included. See, Carl was good at surveillance, and he was almost always ignored, even when he was present. That was the difference between him and the clown. And did he mind having to do all the handy work? Well, sometimes, but shouldn't the buildup be allowed to be fun, too?

Rigatoni Carl, now *he* was the fun guy. Carl snorted out a laugh, smiling into the mirror at the thought as he chewed more of his semi-rancid sandwich.

He reached for the tin of face makeup and plunged his first two fingers into it, removing a glob of white, softly singing to himself as he worked.

The desire to be a clown had started at a very young age. Carl loved the idea of making people laugh, of sharing time with them and making them smile, the feeling of being the personality behind the paint. There was something else to be said as well, the paint being itself a form of transformation for the teen. If Carl was allowed to hide himself away for a bit while others enjoyed the show, well no harm done, right?

The name had soon followed when, as a teen, Carl would replace song lyrics with "Rigatoni Carl" instead of the real ones as a way of passing time at his weekend job. It didn't make any sense, so he had never shared it with anyone else, but it sure did make him laugh. The less sense it made, the funnier it was.

"Whoa, Carl's half way there, whoa-ho, Rigatoni on a prayer," Carl said in a singsong voice.

He continued applying the white makeup, singing as he went, and bit into the second half of his sandwich. The bread had white makeup spread across it in big fingerprints, but he continued to eat it indiscriminately.

As the makeup dried, Carl removed a brush to paint on the traditional diamond eyes. "Today, let's do a purple and a gold!" he called out to no one in particular with a giggle, reaching for the colors.

The closer he got to becoming Rigatoni Carl, the more fun he had. *The fun guy's coming*! ran through his head as he sketched the diamond shape around his eyes in black. For how messy he was with the white, his hands moved with startling dexterity, the lines a near-perfect shape. This was his profession after all, put your best foot forward and all that.

Carl burped loudly and said, "Put your best *food* forward!" The cloying stench of the sandwich meat clung to the air around him.

With one diamond purple and the other gold, Carl sketched an oval around the shape of his lips, laughing and tracing circular motions with lipstick.

He always wondered if other clowns used more paint for the lips or if it was just him. The tube boasted that it was "REAL RED," and the feeling of it was something he couldn't part with. Lips deserved lip products, the real deal. He had even gotten into the habit of putting it on right before bed, without makeup, just to feel a bit closer to Rigatoni, in the hopes that sleep would come. He told the CVS worker that they were for his beloved wife. That always gave him such a good laugh that he was often bent over cackling before he got to his car with his purchase.

"He's here, he's here, HE'S HERE!" Carl chanted in a reverent voice. "Rigatoni Carl is back!"

Carl lowered his face so he could no longer see himself in the mirror. He gave himself time for a few deep breaths before raising his head, becoming.

"Well, hi!" Rigatoni Carl said into the mirror before taking his face and pulling it into various shapes and looks. He took his time with each, practicing. He giggled, coughed, and mimed a crying motion, with his finger running down his face like tears.

"To be honest, I'm just a little sad," Rigatoni Carl said, an over-exaggerated pout pulling his lips. "I'm just a little lonely!" he yelled, following it with a fake sob.

Carl stared at himself in the mirror, his face portraying a dejected, far-off look. The truth was that he was lonely. How could he not be? What he was, who he was, and what he did, how could he not be *alone*?

Of course, that was the doc talking through *Carl*...but no matter, it was Rigatoni's time now.

Another pout in the mirror brought forth a scream of rage. The Clown slapped Carl, hard, hand moving in a comical fashion as Rigatoni tried to bury the man deep within. As fear over his makeup took hold, Rigatoni instead turned to the mirror, punching several times before stopping, watching chunks of glass splinter out onto the bathroom floor.

Rigatoni cackled, and a large smile dragged his lips upward, the rounded lipstick on his face making his smile look like it stretched to his ears. He giggled, reaching for his little clown hat, and snapped it onto his head at a jaunty angle. He stepped back and took himself in, appraising the work done by Carl.

"Ohhhhh, thankfully—thankfully the fun guy is here!" Rigatoni Carl called out, as if his transformation had come just in the nick of time. "He's not wrong though, I am *awfully* lonely. It's time to go grab my newest friend!"

Back then

Carl's father had punched him square in the face. That was his preferred method of saying hello lately. Carl was sixteen and a half and newly unemployed, but the proud owner of his very first set of clown paints. His father had knocked the clown nose right off as he entered the living room.

He was only angry because he didn't have an outlet like this. He didn't have an escape like Carl did. A calling. Ever since Carl's mother had run off with the landlord, his father had only gotten angrier with each consecutive beer. Of which there were many. Cans littered the house in piles and stacks. His ability to maintain a job while drinking so heavily was a magic trick that Carl never wanted to learn.

"Why can't you just be a normal boy? I didn't raise no fucked-up weirdo."

Rigatoni Carl cackled. He bent over as if he was hurt, just to straighten back up with a handful of fake flowers, the bouquet blooming from his sleeve. He offered them to his father, who swatted them away and swung at his son's face again.

Blood leaked from his nose a rosy red. Rigatoni ran his bloody gloved fingers around his lips, drawing the crimson into a wider and wider clown smile.

"I didn't raise no freak. Why can't you be something I can handle? What the fuck is wrong with you, kid? Why couldn't you just be gay?" His father's voice was thick and slowed with drink, yet his punches were anything but. His fists could still hit like a brick. Maybe they were what had chased his mother away. He swung again, screaming derogatory words Carl had never heard said aloud.

Rigatoni Carl froze in mock surprise, head tilting to one side. Anger flared in his made-up eyes. "There's nothing wrong with Carl or gay people," he said, responding to his father for the first time. "But hey, you wanna see another trick?" Rigatoni made a mock show of pulling a pair of brass knuckles from his pocket, playing for an imaginary crowd as he slipped them over his gloved fist.

As the first punch rocked the side of his father's face, Rigatoni Carl smiled gleefully. Blood, spit, and the cracked shards of teeth dribbled down the chin of his blubbering father.

"You know it's not very nice to say those things!" Cackling, and perhaps truly coming unglued for the first time, Rigatoni beat down on his father's face. Blood splattered everything in the living room around them: the TV screen, blaring some midday ballgame, grew unwatchable through globs of red; the ratty recliner, with its end still raised high, exposed the mechanisms to shots of bodily fluids, shards of teeth, and snot; eventually, brain matter found its way to beer cans new and old as Rigatoni rained down his rage.

His father chased his mother away, was always absent, and claimed to be the family workhorse while seemingly never bringing home any money. Worst of all, he never protected Carl, never kept him safe. The bill was past due, and Rigatoni was collecting recompense in blood.

1996

Rigatoni stepped out from behind a thick tree. He was fully transformed now. His pants, one leg houndstooth, the other a colorful plaid, were cuffed right over his oversized, bright-red clown shoes. He wore a suit jacket, the lapels matching his pants, while the arms and panels of the jacket were all different colors: green, red, blue, and yellow. Underneath he wore a startlingly yellow silk vest on top of a black button-up. His bow tie matched his pant legs, the design split directly in the middle and expertly tied.

One thing that his clients—few though they may be—always praised him for was his professionalism. Top notch makeup, clothes, balloons, and props. Rigatoni didn't skimp on anything. It wasn't about money or fame, he simply believed in dressing to impress. Plus, it helped the believability.

Except for that one family that complained that he looked raggedy and smelled. But that had been the longest he had ever gone without Rigatoni. And seriously, he was taking their children off their hands for a literal pittance, what did they expect?

Still, it never failed to amaze him how soon after their children's parties the parents simply forgot him and what he looked like. Just *POOF.* It was as if they weren't paying attention to their children at all!

Rigatoni giggled at the thought.

Parents were never observant. So distracted with their lives, their pagers, and who or what Daddy was going to do after passing the kids back off to their divorcee mother. Anything other than the children. The same rang true even at the playground. "Come back and check with me so I know you're okay, honey," they say so that they can continue on with their own lives without an ounce of guilt. It was fine. Always fine.

Their lack of attention was his gain.

And what a gain it was.

Rigatoni was born because Carl hadn't been kept safe, hadn't been saved. So, the Clown would do for others what couldn't be done for him. He was giving these kids a chance, that's how he saw it. And yes, he did have a propensity for flipping his lid over the slightest occurrences, but he was doing his best.

It had been over three months since Jimmy Costa's little heart had given out on him. Carl had thought he might have been the one, lasting much longer than all the others, but it wasn't meant to be. He had been so strong, even right up until the end. Missing both arms wasn't an easy thing for a kid, especially before they fully developed conversationally. Not to mention Jimmy had been *born* with them. All he had to do was listen, to understand the second chance he had been given—the grace of it even. One escape attempt had landed Jimmy in the basement, where Rigatoni's Bad-Time Room was. The second attempt, though clumsier after losing the first arm, had landed him back in the basement, and the rest was history. Rigatoni didn't consider himself a true vivisectionist, but wasn't it just so much fun? Jimmy had eaten when Rigatoni fed him, drank the offered water, and he had even stopped crying himself to sleep after that. But old boy Carl...he just couldn't stop the infection Jimmy had suffered from.

But where does reminiscing get you?

Rigatoni's new friend, the one that would be living with him after today, was a beautiful little girl named Abby. She came from the same situation as all the others. Her parents couldn't even make it through her party before they had started fighting, loudly and in front of all the kids. Abby had run from the room crying. Rigatoni had been furious. Abby didn't deserve that. She deserved to be with him, the one who would understand her. And they had ruined his never-ending handkerchief bit, one of his favorites. They were so wrapped up in their fight that they didn't even realize Abby had left the room upset. When they did, instead of calming reassurance they reprimanded her, calling her Abigail in front of her friends. She hated her full name. Rigatoni briefly wished that he was interested in adults, the handkerchiefs in his hands itching to be around their necks.

It had all worked out though, and it had been that moment that had solidified her as the next.

Rigatoni watched her playing in her neighborhood's mini playground. She ran back and forth on the Jungle Gym, using the monkey bars and slides. Even though she was the only one there, she shouted in glee every time she descended the slide. Rigatoni couldn't help himself, he giggled with her every time she did it.

All the while, her father sat on the bench before Abby, oblivious, a newspaper opened and completely blocking her from view. This was precisely what got Rigatoni so riled up. Her father was so distracted that he couldn't even see his daughter playing—wasn't being attentive in case of a fall or injury and completely missing her moment of brightness. He couldn't, and didn't, see her—not truly.

Couldn't see her brightly colored assailant for the trees.

Rigatoni watched, and waited, until finally he popped out from behind the tree and waved at Abby. She saw, smiling, and waved back.

She remembered him, she did. Rigatoni felt something come alive within him, burning deep. This, *this*, was why children were so much better than adults. They remembered, they understood. On a certain level, they even believed in him. Rigatoni was going to make Abby such a happy little girl.

Without realizing it, he had started salivating, something unlocking within him, turning on. Something bestial and deep. If her father wanted to make it that easy for him, he might as well go ahead and do it. Abby would be so much happier with him anyway. Rigatoni would be her daddy now.

Would she ever call me Daddy?

Rigatoni didn't think so, but he hoped anyway. Maybe, just maybe.

Stepping through the trees, Rigatoni Carl saw that her father was still engrossed with the newspaper. As soon as Abby went down another slide, her back turned to him, he would make his move. It was finally time. Rigatoni struggled to keep himself from clapping in excitement. Wasn't this just a load of fun?

Abby approached the slide, smiling so brightly a tear came to Rigatoni's eye. It was perfect. So perfect.

It would all be perfect.

As Rigatoni Carl made it to the fence, he placed a white-gloved hand on the cool metal. He was excited enough to jump it, but the fast movement might alert her father.

He scanned their surroundings one last time, left to right. From this side of the fence, there was truly an offensive number of trees. Cover everywhere. His van was parked a quarter of a mile through the woods, in a shaded area off the road.

Rigatoni walked steadily toward the gate, Abby's father still oblivious to anything other than his newspaper.

As he rounded the last bit of fence, Rigatoni heard what sounded like the clicking static of a radio, then the sound of a vehicle tearing down the street. The woods around the bend had given the vehicle just as much cover as Rigatoni.

A van pulled up from out of nowhere, tires screeching and sliding through the gravelly grass.

Abby's father snapped the newspaper shut, standing up and drawing a pistol in quick succession. He hadn't banked on Rigatoni not freezing in surprise, however, and as he looked up, the clown was already upon him.

Rigatoni Carl plunged a nine-inch hunting knife into Abby's father's chest. The pistol dropped to the mulch, completely useless. He sunk the knife home twice more with a *shuck*ing sound. Warm blood soaked through his white gloves and splattered across his painted face. He smiled at the man as he shuddered in pain, his death throes making Rigatoni cackle in his face.

"She's mine, mine, *mine*," Rigatoni Carl called in the dying man's face, a ball of excitement. He had never killed the parent before. He liked it. As Abby's father crumpled, Rigatoni grabbed him by the shoulders, taking in his dead face and lowering him back to the bench below.

But wait...that was *not* Abby's daddy. The Clown stared down into a face he didn't recognize. It should have stood out as odd—if he was so engrossed in the paper why hadn't he seemed to be reading it? No pages turned, no mumbled commentary. Rigatoni had been too locked in, too excited to slow himself down.

The bastards had set Rigatoni up! That wasn't how it was supposed to happen.

A stream of officers jumped from the van. Now that it wasn't screeching up out of nowhere, Rigatoni could clearly see the matte-black 'POLICE' along the side of it. Had he been less careful than he had thought? Did that moments-long stare at the high school now hold meaning? Had they been onto him for years? This opened a whole slew of possibilities he'd never imagined.

"Freeze!" multiple officers shouted at once, guns raised in his direction.

An officer approached Rigatoni, pistol pointed at his chest. "Slowly lower your knife to the ground and kick it toward me." When Rigatoni Carl made no move to comply, the officer screamed "Now!" and gesticulated with the raised firearm.

Rigatoni tilted his head to the side, as if he was trying to understand what the officer had said. He looked down, taking in his bloody gloves and splattered outfit. He tossed the knife away, miming his movements to the officers. He skipped over to the dead officer on the bench, pretending to kill him all over again before bending over and laughing hysterically.

"Wasn't this just a load of fun?" he asked in between gasping breaths. He sat on the bench and wrapped an arm around the dead man, pulling him in tight, before bouncing back up to the balls of his feet.

Rigatoni Carl slowly turned his head in the hopes of not startling the officers into action. He tried to look back at his dear Abby. He had come too close to not get to be with her now.

She stood only feet from him, no longer on the Jungle Gym, and so close that he could smell her strawberry shampoo in the breeze. She would have been the perfect one. He just knew it.

Then they had to go and ruin everything.

Rigatoni shouted and lunged toward her, his only hope to hold her at least a single time. Just once.

Two gunshots reverberated around the surrounding trees in what should have been a shocking amount of noise.

Rigatoni Carl heard none of it, stumbling forward. He sunk to his knees, blood already soaking through his clown clothes and into the playground mulch. All he could see was the spray of blood across Abby's face.

His blood.

Abby's face was in shock, pale with eyes glazed over.

Rigatoni Carl collapsed into the mulch, his face pressed into the dirt. As his breath began to catch, his blood soaking more of the ground than his insides, the truth finally hit him.

This hadn't been fun at all.

CHUPABOGRA

August 15, 2006

The summer sun beat down as five best friends searched for shade. Colin's mother had dropped him off at Andy's, and Andy's mother had dropped them off at Iain's hours ago. Tommy and Brandon had biked over, but Iain's mother didn't want them all crowding around the house. Not on her day off, not if she could help it.

She'd been making comments like that a lot lately. The family's old, beaten-up leather sectional had been home to many a sleep over, the boys finding comfort in the black leather like it was a second home. Late-night pizzas and Blockbuster rentals giving way to less frequent invites. And lately, Iain's mother would roll her eyes and tell them they needed to enjoy the outdoors, and suddenly they weren't so welcome anymore. The group thought Iain's parents might be getting a divorce. Iain would never talk about it though. Even warned them to keep quiet about it, too.

The boys made their way down Orchard Street, trees pregnant with green leaves hung heavy over powerlines and the sunbaked pavement causing a puddle-like inferior mirage to form around the bend. Doing their best to stay on the side of the road, they flipped off any cars passing too closely. A mix of thirteen and fourteen, this was their final summer before entering high school. Their desire to appear cool trumped the manners their parents tried to instill in them. As a group, they presented themselves as tough guys, but the façade would be tested soon enough.

Colin was short, his belly growing pudgy in recent years. He hid behind band shirts and hoodies, buying up the entire Chiodos online store in hopes of camouflaging his growing weight. Andy was dealing with a similar situation; however, he was taller, wearing the weight better. He wore the tightest skinny jeans money could buy. Brandon was tall, constantly in need of a good meal, and had such blonde hair that the sunshine seemed to erase his hairline. No matter the season he always wore long sleeves. Tommy was the shortest. The kind of short that held out for a growth spurt, promising themselves they'd hit six feet one day. His personality was often dominated by the chip on his shoulder at being the runt of the group. Iain was the coolest by far, his voice deepening the quickest. Muscular and above average in height, he purposefully wore t-shirts that were too small, making his biceps bulge through the shirtsleeves.

Boredom and Iain's temperamental mother forced them out into the neighborhood. As is the plight of young teens, they couldn't drive yet, therefore they'd gotten used to walking all over God's green earth to make it to their destinations. Due to the summer heat, they were all open to taking shortcuts. These shortcuts were often longer than the original route, but if it led them off the busy road, the extra distance was well worth the sense of adventure.

The boys broke off from the street and headed down an embankment, hopping over the pitiful stream that piddled along. They clambered up the other side, leading up behind the back of a maintenance building. The ten-foot concrete wall was lined so closely by a fence they had to bend and contort their bodies to fit between it. Minutes later, as the final boy pulled himself from the fence, Iain led them off through the trees. Iain had a way of leading that the others simply accepted, not that he would have allowed himself to be challenged. One time Colin thought he was simply being funny, but he later received an AIM instant message from Iain stating that if he wanted to be in charge they should fistfight for it. Colin had stayed quiet since, stayed wary too.

Colin noticed Iain kept them going to the right, past the wall and off into the thickening trees. There was no trail for him to follow, but he walked with purpose. This stuck out as odd since to Colin's knowledge that was an uncharted region for the group. He supposed if they cut far enough it would lead back to the main road, but that seemed an awful lot of work just to end up having to walk all the way back. There wasn't even anything cool to see, but as Colin wasn't the leader, he remained tight-lipped.

An hour later, they walked out of the woods into an unfamiliar neighborhood...well, the backside of one. The row of backyards was blocked off by an ever-extending fence. The people of Cemetery loved their fences, but the boys often just jumped them. Rather than an actual deterrent, they were simply an obstacle for the boys to conquer.

A putrid stench hit them as they rounded the last backyard. An oddly sweet, sickly scent that drove the boys to gagging. Iain urged them on, leading them toward the smell. In a dense copse of trees, the boys could just make out the vague shape of something lying in the dead leaves. They edged closer, cautiously, toward the silhouette in the shade. Colin pressed the collar of his shirt over his mouth and nose, moving slower than the other boys. His mother always said he had a sympathetic stomach. It was a kind way of describing his predisposition to vomiting at a moment's notice. He did his best to distance himself without appearing to do so, hoping to avoid Iain's judgment.

Iain laughed as he made it to the source of the putrid smell, kicking whatever it was. The others laughed as well, but with varying degrees of enthusiasm. Tommy and Brandon seemed interested, Andy looked uneasy, and Colin was positively green.

As Colin leaned over and vacated his lunch, Iain called out, "Feast your eyes on dinner, boys!"

Colin vomited again in quick succession.

The carcass of a deer lay before them, one that had been dead for quite some time judging by the state of decay. The smell was enough to push anyone over the edge, but what was worse were the eyes, or lack thereof. They were simply gone. Rotten or eaten. The thought made Colin heave again. The boys looked at the deer, taking in all its liquifying glory. The eyes weren't the only horror; the top of the skull was caved in, and the stomach had a yawning, gaping hole in it, as did the rectum. Maybe devoured by time or something more.

"What the hell could do something like that?" Colin tried to sound in control, but his voice cracked midsentence.

Brandon's voice was deeper, steady. "I heard bears eat things from the ass up because it's an easy access point." He kicked a rock, looking mildly embarrassed to have volunteered such weird information, but still sporting a smirk.

"Could a bear do that? This thing is obliterated," Colin replied. "Look at it, that's not just eaten, it's...destroyed."

Silence passed between the group.

Eventually, the morbid interest all adolescent boys possess began to wane. Three of them wandered off, but not far enough to be out of earshot.

Colin walked in expanding loops, distancing himself for the sake of his gag reflex. He didn't want to appear weak, but he was tired of dry heaving. He had the creeping suspicion Iain was keeping them there just to humiliate him.

Colin made his largest loop yet, stumbling upon a clearing in the trees. There was a medium-sized swath of flat dirt, bone-dry from the rays of beating sun. Taking care to avoid dirtying his Nike Dunks, he noticed a set of prints. From what animal though, he had no clue.

"Uhh, hey guys," Colin called loudly over their distant conversation. "Come take a look at this."

Colin let the hot summer air hang between them until Iain finally shrugged and sauntered over, the rest at his heels.

"They're just animal prints," Tommy squeaked. "And we are in the *woods*."

"But what kind of animal?" Andy asked.

"Rabbits make that kind of print," Brandon replied, pointing, "with the sort of elongated slide on the back from them hopping."

Iain gave him a look and said, "why do you know this shit, you *NatGeo* nerd?"

"How big do rabbits get?" Colin interrupted, voice growing shaky. He wanted to interject so that Brandon wouldn't take the bait, but he didn't want the attention either.

"Uh, around here? Probably not very big," Brandon answered.

"Okay, so it's not a rabbit then, dumbass," Iain said. "Those prints are at least the size of my feet."

The boys let the statement settle over them. They could all see it. One paw print spanned a bigger surface area than most of their own feet, sneakers included. What could it be?

What could have done that to the deer?

What could it do to one of *them*?

One of their cellphones *ding*ed, making them collectively jump. Tommy shoved Brandon to ease the tension. Andy pulled his phone from his pocket, flipping it open and looking at the text.

"Shit, my mom wants me home for dinner."

"Mine told me she did too," Tommy said.

Iain could tell he was losing them. "Come on you babies, don't you want to know what the hell this is? We gotta find this thing,"

"Alright, dude, yeah," Colin said, playing cool. Before he even opened his mouth though, the weighing sense of dread was thick. "Uhh, why don't we meet back up later. Cover of darkness or whatever, maybe we'll see something?"

"Fuck yeah, Colin! Okay," Iain said. "Now you're thinking."

AT NINE THAT NIGHT, the boys were to meet back up at Iain's parents' house. He had sent a text telling them to bring a weapon and a flashlight. Tommy was mysteriously no longer allowed out after they received the text. Colin assumed his mom had read it. Iain assumed it was because he was scared.

It was whatever anyway, Iain said; Tommy was a pussy.

Colin showed up early hoping to avoid attracting Iain's ire by being empty-handed. He searched around the top of the street until he found half of a smashed vodka bottle with jagged edges. Andy had a broken surveyor's stake, the wooden kind with an orange spray-painted top. It was snapped into the perfect point. Iain had a long bike chain wrapped around his right fist, the excess hanging toward the ground like a whip. Brandon had a switchblade that the other boys practically drooled over. All shining steel with a black carbon fiber handle. It reminded Colin of the one he'd seen in English class when Ms. Ritter showed them *The Outsiders*. Colin had loved the book also, and although they agreed it sucked after class, he'd been glued to the screen.

Back in the woods, they followed the path they had taken hours earlier. The waning gibbous moon hung high, giving off decent light until they got deeper into the trees. If help was needed, it would be a long way away.

It was a particularly humid night, the boys' shirts sticking to their bodies as they trekked back to the fenced neighborhood. The woods were alive with the sounds of owls, crickets, and the rustling of leaves and branches in the sticky breeze.

The teens felt invincible with their weapons. It didn't matter how makeshift they were (save for Brandon's); this was what being tough was all about, the projection of it. At least that's what it meant to them. The feeling that no one would mess with them. The projected sense of power, however imagined, was incredible.

None of them ever thought they'd be put to the test.

When they reached the copse of trees from earlier, the animal's remains were gone. Like it had never been there at all. They searched: blood, hair, gore, but there was nothing. Iain grew impatient as the boys swore the location was correct. It didn't matter, he assured them, they'd keep looking even if there wasn't a trail.

No one argued.

A mile or so into their investigation they came upon a huge hill. The bottom of the slope dropped off at a severe angle into a small stream. However, the opposite bank looked to be only a few bounds to crest. There were sparse saplings on either side, a much cooler breeze coming off the running water. But what drew the boys toward it was the gigantic drainage tunnel that led off through the end of the stream. Decrepit concrete lined the sides to keep the rainwater from traveling back out, and fencing covered the perimeter.

The boys hurriedly slid down the hill. Colin, finally having enough of the humidity, plopped himself on a rock beside the stream. He placed the smashed bottle down, sinking the edges into the muck. Facing the drainage tunnel, he noted with a hint of dread that Iain would likely lead them there next. He wished he'd just stayed home. Iain would've called him a pussy too, but at least he wouldn't be soaked in sweat struggling through the woods. And at least he'd be shamed alongside Tommy instead of alone. He'd finally convinced his parents to get him *Guild Wars* for his birthday, and despite all the hours spent gaming, he had yet to beat it.

Deep down though Colin knew tonight would bump him a smidge above Tommy in Iain's favor and for that, the sweat was worth it. The friend group's ever-changing hierarchy bothered him, but there wasn't much to be done about it while Iain was in charge. They were all vying for a spot near the top, not to mention the genuine satisfaction of seeing their rank change among Iain's MySpace Top 8. He wondered, and not for the first time, if that desire to be the "best" friend was just so that they could feel the safest. However fleeting it was.

Colin felt ill. His shirt stuck to him in an all-too familiar way, reminiscent of last week when Iain shoved him into Andy's pool fully clothed. The shirt suctioned to his body to the point that he thought they'd need scissors to remove it. Iain claimed it was an accident, but Colin knew better.

As predicted, Iain had already scrambled ahead to the pitch-black mouth of the tunnel. He stuck his head inside before excitedly calling the boys over. "Look at this thing! It's big enough that we'll only have to crouch down a little, won't even get our shoes wet." He ducked inside, gesturing for them to follow.

"I'm just catching my breath, Andy," Colin called. "Tell Iain I'll be right there."

Andy gave him a sympathetic glance before plunging into the darkness.

Colin sat, savoring the semi-cool breeze blowing against his sweat-slicked back. An errant curl fell into his eye, and he brushed it away before it began soaking up sweat from his forehead. He could hear his friends talking on the other side of the tunnel. Either the sound was carrying, or the tunnel was smaller than it looked. Colin almost heard them perfectly, the only distortion coming off the running water.

A sound off to the side drew his attention. Was that a branch snapping? Weren't they like three miles into the woods or something? Shouldn't they be alone?

Maybe it was just a rabbit like Brandon said?

Maybe Tommy had changed his mind and was just now catching up?

Colin whipped his head around, scanning the trees before him. He heard it again, another crack. Ice entered his bloodstream, spread its way through his body in chills, making him wish for the heat from before.

He could still hear his friends talking on the other side of the tunnel, so who was coming toward him? Who—or *what*?

"Andy, are you messing with me?" Colin called. He tried to keep his voice from quavering.

In lieu of an answer came another snapping branch, this time much closer. Colin frantically pawed through his backpack looking for the flashlight. His eyes went wide as if begging for enough moonlight to see.

Where the hell was the damn thing? There were only like seven items in the bag, and yet he was struggling to find it. Panic sank its teeth into him as he continued to rummage.

There!

Finally, his hand grasped the flashlight. He drew it out and flicked it on, his arm outstretched toward the approaching sounds. At first, he saw nothing: just leaves, branches, dirt, an old iTunes gift card—the detritus of woods. As seconds turned to painstaking minutes, Colin continued to pan the flashlight back and forth.

Another snapping branch drew Colin's eye to the left. What he saw caused him to drop the flashlight. With little more than a *splish*, it was swept downstream. With a scream, he gripped the half vodka bottle for dear life and sprinted for the drainage tunnel.

He sloshed through the surprisingly cold ankle-deep water, too consumed by fear to care for his Dunks any longer. All that mattered was reaching the end. Reaching his friends.

As Colin exited the tunnel, he was met by three shocked faces. They took him in—disheveled, pale, sweatier than ever, and wild-eyed.

"Holy crap, guys," Colin yelled. "There—there was something over there! I saw something, kind of like a leg, but it—it wasn't normal."

Iain's smirk was dripping with disbelief. Leaning forward, he said, "Quit whining and tell us what the hell you're talking about, man."

"Well, I kept hearing these snapping branches, like I wasn't alone. So, I got my flashlight out and saw something step out from behind a tree. It looked like a hairy leg, but like, furry, not a human leg. But it was still upright like a human's." Colin looked around at his friends. From one set of disbelieving eyes to another. "You've got to believe me; I swear I saw it."

Iain opened his mouth, most likely to say something snarky, but never got the chance. A ruckus came from the end of the tunnel. It sounded as if something was cracking a giant tree.

The noise alone ended the debate. The boys looked at each other, fear or shock on every face. The noise came ever closer to the tunnel entrance.

"You're bleeding," Andy said, pointing to Colin's hand.

Colin let the half vodka bottle's neck slide in his sweaty palm. He must have done it scrambling away from the stream, the glass so sharp he hadn't even noticed the cut.

SMASH! The noise was just feet away. Whatever was in the tunnel was almost upon them.

Colin dropped the vodka bottle. It fell to the ground, splintering into a million tiny shards. He'd taken off at a run before the bottle had even landed. His friends followed, coming out of their shock one at a time.

Colin ran full tilt through the fenced in area. Unlike the neighborhood earlier, this area seemed devoid of human life. The ground declined gradually, helping him break his typical max speed. But the further he ran the ground grew damper, the area thick with seven-foot-tall cattails.

A swamp in the middle of the woods? The wetlands were miles away, closer to the Hudson River. It had been a particularly dry summer, too.

What was this place?

The group ran frantically for what felt like an hour. Eventually their adrenaline petered out. They stopped together, panting and bent forward, with hands on knees.

"What the hell was that, Colin?" Iain asked, his tone accusatory.

"How the hell should I know? Just because I saw it first doesn't make me the leading expert on it or something," Colin said, pressing his bleeding hand into the bottom of his sweaty Chiodos shirt. "Do you guys think it's the thing that left those prints and killed the deer? And why is there a fenced-in swamp in the middle of the woods?"

Brandon straightened, wiping his dripping forehead with the back of a sweatshirt sleeve. "It looked like the thing was leaping after us for a while. Whenever I looked back, it seemed like it was clipping through the tops of the cattails, but I couldn't see it clearly." He took a deep breath. "Also, this isn't really a swamp."

The boys looked at Brandon like he was crazy.

"I just mean that swamps are, by definition, typically around large lakes and rivers. That little stream back there's not cutting it...even when there isn't a summer drought."

"Call it a freaking bog for all I care, Brandon," Colin wailed. "What the hell, dude! We gotta get out of here!"

The rustling sound came again, in front of them this time. The boys looked at each other.

"It circled around us. What the fuck could have done that so fast? What the hell is this thing?" Iain said, smacking his bike-chained fist into his palm in challenge.

In front of them, the boys saw the swaying and dipping of cattails as whatever was chasing them drew nearer. It looked like it was bounding toward them.

All four stared in fear, frozen. Paralyzed by the panic, not one of them was able to move a muscle.

As the rustling reached its peak—the noise as close to them as each other—the cattails parted. *Something* jumped through. The boys, with mouths agape, tried to take in what they were seeing, its fast movement, the lack of light, and their heightened paranoia making whatever it was a blur.

The beast completed its dive, spinning midair and raking gangrenous claws across Iain's back before hitting the ground. Its talons reflected in the scattered flashlight beams, dripping blood, before it disappeared back into the brush.

Iain screamed in pain; a sound so raw it was unlike any they'd ever heard. He stumbled forward and fell to his knees, bike chain long forgotten.

Brandon stepped forward, hand digging into his sweatshirt pocket. He raised a small snub-nosed revolver, firing twice after the thing as the others stared in abject terror.

"Where did you get a freaking gun?" Andy and Colin asked in concert.

The switchblade had been one thing, but an entire *loaded* firearm? This had nothing to do with appearing tough. Colin wondered just who the hell he was hanging out with.

"My dad leaves his stuff unlocked," Brandon said with a shrug. "Does it really matter right now? RUN!" He gingerly helped Iain stand, keeping the revolver raised. He squinted through the cattails. "It's like a freaking maze out here!"

Iain groaned, raising his left hand over his shoulder and feeling the damage done. He winced each time his fingers connected with the slashes. There were tears in his eyes that he refused to shed. "Yeah, let's go."

The rustling started up again, this time from another direction. Wordlessly the boys struck out in what they took to be the opposite way. Water splashed beneath them as they pushed and pulled their way through the dense thicket. Every other step was an obstacle, the cattails whipping against their skin. The sounds of swishing and swaying followed in their wake.

They struggled through for what felt like the entire night. The sky remained stubbornly dark above them, letting them know that they weren't done just yet. The group continued, occasionally tripping and helping each other up.

Finally, they broke into a clearing. The area around them was void of trees, cattails, or water. There appeared to be something at the end of the clearing, but the boys were too far to make heads or tails of it.

Iain motioned for them to continue forward. They spread out, edging their way toward whatever laid beyond. Colin walked as close to his friend as he could, Andy's makeshift weapon held aloft like a spear.

They neared the end of the clearing. To remain alert, their flashlight beams skated frantically over every square inch of space. What they previously couldn't make out was finally before them. It was some kind of structure. Crude for certain, but it appeared to be a hut, or perhaps a cave or alcove. Broken and bent branches and cattails were deliberately shaped into some sort of...home. The branches were layered, with fresher, leafier ones laid over top. The bottom of the dwelling was lined with moss and leaves, and while it was made from decaying nature, it appeared neat, even well-kept. It was noticeably dry inside, and they could see pictures, or at least attempts at them, although many were upside down or at odd angles. Many were old company brochures or faded newspaper, but a few celebrities could be made out too. What looked like ancient holiday lights were woven into the front of the structure. This must be the beast's base of operations.

Colin's mind raced as puzzle pieces clicked together. It had a bed. It decorated. It *lived* here. This thing, which had shown some semblance of intelligence, had built itself a place to stay. But what the hell was it? Was that why it was fenced in? If the stream wasn't so dry from the hot summer, the drainage tunnel would be nearly impassable...

Andy's spear dropped to the ground. "It led us to its freaking house?"

"Wait—wait, where's Brandon?" Colin asked, looking back and finding he wasn't there.

"He was the one with the gun!" Andy said. "We're screwed, man."

"What the hell is this thing, a monster? A Chupacabra?" Iain asked.

"Aren't they supposed to be weird little vampire-fanged things that prey on sheep?" Colin replied.

"Okay, then a—a fucking Chupa*bog*ra?"

Before any retort could be made, Iain fell forward onto dirtied knees. His face looked pained, his eyes wild. He looked at them both, as if for help, before wrenching his body into a freakish shape, his skin tightening and stretching too far. Black and green ooze seeped from his shoulder wound and mouth. Screams escaped him as he fell flat to the ground, seizing.

Something was happening. Iain was changing.

Even through Colin's shock, his panic, he wondered if Iain was truly transforming, or if the scratch from the monster simply allowed his true self to be released. As if the sloughing off of skin was just helping to expose the rot already hidden beneath.

The beast jumped over the impossibly tall cattails, landing in a roll and stopping on all fours. Its face was dark, drooping, with a fanged snout that caught in the moonlight. A layer of fir lined its body, and its muscular chest heaved with exertion. It had arms that were unnaturally long, stretching from its thick shoulders to where they pawed at the ground.

It stood, hunching forward, and brandished sharp claws. While Iain still convulsed on the ground, Colin thought that he saw something oddly similar in their features even pre-change, but tendrils of panic had latched onto him, slowing his processing.

Hoping to stop the beast from coming any closer, Andy threw his makeshift spear at it. For a moment it sailed through the air, appearing as if it would hit its mark. At the last possible second, a clawed hand snatched the spear from its flight, applying pressure and disintegrating it as if it had been nothing more than a termite-infested toothpick.

Finished changing, or perhaps becoming, Iain raised his newly monstrous body from the ground. The noise that escaped him was guttural, inhuman. He locked eyes with the other beast, a pregnant pause stilling the air in the clearing. All the boys' hair stood on end, then the beasts lunged.

The boys screamed.

DON'T SCREAM

Phone Calls from Home

Callie stood in the kitchen, twirling a curl of her hair and leaning over the island. Popcorn spun oily circles in the microwave, popping wildly, and water boiled on the stovetop for hot chocolate or tea. She hadn't yet decided which. Her other hand fiddled with half a pencil, tapping it against a Sudoku book. She was terrible at them but wanted to distract herself while she waited, so had grabbed the first thing she saw.

The marble island burned cold against her skin, her too-short shirt leaving just the littlest bit of skin exposed against the absorbent stone. The hardwood floor felt good against her bare feet, but as the counter sapped her warmth, she figured it was time to get her slippers on.

Callie had just turned seventeen. A rising senior at Cemetery High School. A bright future ahead of her. At least that's what everyone kept telling her. It's not that she disagreed, she just felt like there was so much self-awakening left. So much to experience. With parents so strict she didn't even have a cellphone, everything seemed dull. All of her friends had had them since they were like eight years old. She felt like a bird trapped in an ever-shrinking cage when all she wanted to do was fly.

Her parents were so strict they even had the TV and laptops set with an age lock—score one for mom and dad raising a perpetual twelve-year-old. If that was what they aimed to do, they were really knocking it out of the park.

As if watching horror, violence, or sex had ever warped someone's mind before.

She had taken to going to her boyfriend Miles' house to binge watch horror movies in secret. New and old. Good and bad. Didn't matter. She loved it all. Her parents thought they had an unspoken agreement with Miles' parents, but truth be told, they were polar opposites. No restrictions there.

She struggled with failing yet another sudoku puzzle. To be fair, the book belonged to her father, and the cover did read "for experts." Even though she was certainly not one, she still felt oddly stupid. Furiously tapping the half pencil against the book in thought, she was too absorbed to notice the kettle coming to a boil. The squealing release of pressure screamed at the same moment the microwave beeped its completion. Callie yelped, and jumped.

Callie rushed to the stove and pulled the kettle off the heat. Turning off the burner, she slumped against the counter, her heart rate slowly returning to normal.

Had she really been so easily spooked?

Tea it is. Chamomile, too.

She grabbed the box out of the cabinet above the stove and plopped a bag into a fresh mug before pouring the steaming water over it. Sliding the mug onto the island, she crossed the kitchen to get a bowl for the popcorn. Miles preferred to simply have at it, but the idea of sticking her hand into a buttery, oily bag over and over seemed barbaric.

Callie had just made it into the hall, bowl and steaming mug in hand, when the housephone rang. She jumped again, steaming tea and buttery popcorn flying all over her. Her scream cut short as the hot tea stung through her shirt. She leaned forward as quickly as she could and ripped the shirt over her head with a curse, the hot fabric grazing her forehead.

The phone continued to ring off the hook all the while.

Callie disappeared into the hall closet before returning in a pullover hoodie. Crisis averted, she ran for the phone.

Her parents were so old school. It was like living on the prairie. Like, they wouldn't even consider a *portable* house phone. Just the heinously tangled and long-corded phone attached to the wall. A less annoyed Callie might have thought of how on-brand that was for horror films, but she was beside herself.

Snagging the phone off the hook and letting it rest in the crook of her neck, Callie said, "Hello, Sanderson residence."

Her hello was met with heavy breathing. Gasping, wheezing breaths raked through the receiver. Callie held the phone away from her ear and repeated her "hello." When no response came, Callie slammed the phone onto the hook, blood pumping in irritation.

Stepping away, Callie did her best to shake off the phone call. The creeps too. She used her foot to mop her wet t-shirt through the rest of the tea on the floor. Just as she finished, the phone rang again.

She had a mind to let it ring until they were satisfied no one would answer. For a moment she did, but the noise always grated her nerves.

Back in the kitchen she grabbed the phone, yelling, "What do you want?"

"Now, I don't think that's any way to answer the phone, young lady," Callie's mother said.

Damn it!

"Sorry, Mom," Callie tried desperately. "Some weirdo just called and—and they were breathing all heavy and not saying anything. It was really gross and creeped me out."

"A weirdo on the phone?" her mother replied, voice rife with incredulity. "We will have to discuss this later. I'm just calling to warn you I'm stuck at work again. Can you order a pizza or something? Your father is stuck at the firehouse, too. I don't know when we'll be home."

Callie thanked her mother for the heads-up. This had become their new normal, her parents preoccupied while she rotted on the couch. It felt like her mother always perfectly timed her calls so they were just late enough to keep her daughter from making plans. Just another form of caging her.

The phone had barely settled its weight back onto the hook before it rang again. Callie grabbed for it, figuring her mother had forgotten something.

"Yeah, Mom?"

"What's your favorite horror movie?" a brusque voice said in response. It was grainy and modulated, as if the person spoke through something.

"Who is this?" Callie said, staring at the phone in disgust, as if she could convey the feeling through the telephone line.

"Is it *Halloween*?"

"*Thirteen Ghosts*?"

"*Cabin Fever*?"

Callie's fear rose with each question, but then an idea took shape.

"Miles, is that you? Because it isn't funny, you're creeping me out. What the hell did you do to your voice?"

"Is it *Dead Silence*?"

"Miles, stop it!" Callie begged.

"How about this...if you don't answer me, I'll come cut you to bloody ribbons. We'll make our own fucking horror movie, huh, how's that sound, bitch?"

Tears sprang at the corners of Callie's eyes. They carved salty rivers down her face as her eyes widened. Miles would *not* talk to her like that. Who could it be on the other end?

"I'll just hang up and call the police, you freaking creep!"

"Do that and I'll come cut up your mother instead! How's that sound for a trade off?"

"You leave my family alone!" Callie was crying outright, hand shaking as it held the phone to her ear. This was going exactly how it did in the movies. Callie could *not* be a victim. She had finally gotten to senior year, the best one in high school. Miles and her were doing so well, she was sure they'd stay together when they left for college. This couldn't be happening.

"You don't want to play? All right then."

The line went dead, the staticky sound of silence ringing in her ear as she numbly held the phone. Callie's whole body felt numb save for the pulsing panic coursing through her system.

Forcing movement, Callie slammed the phone down on the hook. In the hopes of getting her mother again, she grabbed it right back up. A warning. A plea. Perhaps both.

Callie held the dead phone in shock. She pumped the hook up and down, hoping the cradle was stuck, but the line was completely dead. She stared at the phone in her hand, the panic radiating up to the top of her scalp, sweat breaking out on her forehead.

The sound of a door creaking broke Callie from her stupor. It sounded almost as if it had come from upstairs...but Callie was home alone.

Completely alone.

Callie slid forward on the hardwood floor, tugging hard on a drawer in the kitchen island. It always got stuck. Finally, she was able to fidget with it enough to get it open halfway. She grasped a chef's knife by the handle, brandishing it in both hands.

With shaking limbs that felt like Jell-O, she tiptoed her way to the hall. "Dad? Did you just get home?"

Please, please, please be Dad.

A creak from the landing upstairs drew Callie's eyes. At the railing stood a figure dressed in black robes, with a round hood pulled snugly over their head. Callie wasn't sure if they were a tall, imposing figure, or if it was because they were so high above her, but they were terrifying.

She screamed.

The face of the figure snapped down to stare directly at Callie. Tears streamed steadily as she took in the masked face. It was gaunt, overly rounded, white, and nearly transparent. Like a layer of smoke over the real face below it. Callie screamed again, frozen in fear and unable to move an inch as the robed figure descended the stairs toward her.

As the figure reached the last few steps, Callie broke from her immobility. In her haste to get away, she dropped the knife. It skidded across the floor as she ran for the kitchen.

The robed figure followed, only briefly pausing to retrieve the knife. They chased Callie in circles around the island, swinging the knife in wild arcs and knocking random items to the floor. Battered glass and severed bananas tumbled to the hardwood, getting stomped under heavy boots.

The two feigned left and right, neither actually moving. The endless loop caused Callie's stomach to drop in anticipation of what came next. Callie was caught on the farthest side from the hall. The masked figure laughed in their modulated voice, jeering at her, adding an extra step each way as they feigned.

"So, what's your favorite horror movie, Callie-girl?" the voice pressed. "What's it gonna be?"

Again she was caged. A different perpetrator, the same claustrophobic punishment. When would she finally stand up for herself? Break free?

Callie took a ragged inhale of breath, tears still streaming, and ran to the right. However, the attacker was ready, running full tilt in the same direction as Callie, mere seconds from catching her.

Callie spun on the spot, twisting her ankle and catching herself on the island. Hobbling to the left, she went as fast as her limp would allow. The attacker slowed, mocking her with lazy swipes of the knife. Callie backed away from the strikes, eyes on the weapon.

As she rounded the final corner between the island and freedom, Callie placed her full weight onto her back foot—right into shattered glass. Callie bit down on her lip to keep from falling over, the result of which would only put more glass into her.

Twisting, Callie leapt over the remaining glass, taking care to extend her uncut foot. Landing just clear of the shards, she did her best to sprint into the remainder of the house.

As she made it to the stairs, Callie's bloody foot slipped out from under her. The robed figure closed the distance. Callie clawed her way up the stairs, pulling her weight with the carpet runner.

The masked attacker grabbed at her foot with their free hand, latching onto her ankle and pulling hard. Callie struggled against the attacker's grip, flailing wildly. Blood pounded through her ears, drowning out the modulated gibes.

With a frantic kick, Callie dislodged the gloved hand from her ankle. Landing a hard kick to the attacker's eerie mask, Callie sliced the glass further into her foot, blood flowing freely.

Momentarily stunned, the attacker fell backward limply, allowing Callie to scramble the rest of the way up the stairs. Crossing the threshold of her bedroom, she slammed the door shut, twisting the lock. With shaking fingers, she tore the piece of glass from her foot, a geyser of blood spurting out in response. She tossed it across the room.

She tried to shuffle her chest of drawers over to the door, but when it wouldn't budge, she gave up.

Cowering behind her bed, Callie faced the door, waiting with bated breath for the attacker. She needed a weapon, to find something to fight with, but knew there was nothing good in here.

Callie said a rushed prayer as the door handle jiggled. It held. A body slammed into the door as the attacker's patience ran dry. The door hinges clicked back and forth between shouldering blasts to the door and frame. As the door's lock gave way, Callie begged for mercy, for grace, for forgiveness to slights both imagined and real.

The masked figure stared at her as they strode into the room.

"Wait, wait!" Callie shook. "Why are you doing this?"

"You should have just answered the fucking question," the modulated voice said.

"What is this, you—you freak?" Callie tried to run past them, but they grabbed her, tossing her onto the bed.

She twisted onto her back, staring up at them in terror. She put her hands up as if she could stop whatever came next. She thought of begging again, but nothing came from her mouth.

Stepping forward, the masked assailant loomed overhead. They enjoyed inching closer, watching her shake and cry under them. Her mouth was open in a frozen grimace, her eyes locked in terror, the whites showing as tears ran down into her curly hair. Black-gloved hands dramatically raised the knife over their head before plunging it toward her chest.

Callie rolled, her muscles screaming in protest. The kitchen knife sunk into the mattress up to the handle. Callie screamed again, scrambling to the edge of the bed. The assailant struggled with the knife, which must have been stuck between the mattress coils. Callie kicked them hard with her good foot, causing them to drop to the floor.

She wasted no time, sprinting down the hall toward the stairs. If she could just reach the door, could reach freedom. Could escape the cage. Get help.

Just a bit farther!

She slipped and skidded awkwardly along the hardwood floor of the landing, the limp becoming more prevalent with each step. She just had to hold out a little longer.

Almost there!

The masked assailant exited her bedroom as Callie made it to the top of the stairs. They jumped and skipped over her bloody prints, running straight for her as she started the slow work of limping down the stairs, leaning upon the railing.

Callie had only made it down the first two when the attacker crashed into her back. The knife went spinning over the railing, and the two of them rolled and thrashed together down the remaining steps.

As they reached the bottom, Callie's head hit the floor with a deafening crack. She saw stars and closed her eyes, hoping they'd go away and that the room would stop spinning. She tried to sit up, but the hall spread out before her like a kaleidoscope. As she dropped her head back to the floor, she heard the attacker shuffling around her. Their movements were slower now. She must not be the only one hurt.

They limped past her, heading for the knife. Callie lolled her head, throwing her arms wide in an attempt to catch their ankles. Anything to give herself a chance. She latched on, weakly gripping the robes at their heel, barely strong enough to hang on.

"No!" Callie screamed.

They kicked, trying to release her hold, but she managed to stay attached. They leaned forward, stepping in a lunge, and reached across the floor for the knife. Their gloved fingers tapped against the knife's handle, just out of reach.

The attacker yelled in anger, the sound screeching through the modulator. They turned swiftly, landing a punch to Callie's ribs. The shock of pain through her abdomen sent her head reeling. Her hands dropped to her midsection.

Callie groaned, fighting for air. How much more could she take of the abuse before she was finished? She struggled, putting every ounce of her might into getting to her knees.

The smoke-faced assailant stood before her, the kitchen knife back in their gloved fist. They stared down at her, the mask a ghostly, transparent fright. Their breath came heavy, labored and intense. They gripped the knife. Callie imagined white knuckles under gloves.

This couldn't be how she died, right?

The attacker raised the knife above their head again.

Callie waited for the right moment, then struck.

With all her might, Callie punched the masked figure in the groin, driving her fist so hard that she thought she heard something pop. The air left them in an audible *woosh*, and they collapsed backward. The knife clattered to the floor.

Springing into action, Callie leapt on top of her attacker. She pressed their arms to the floor with her knees, using her weight and their weakened state against them. She reached for the knife, holding it threateningly above their stomach. With her left hand, she leaned forward and gripped the mask.

As she stared down at the battered face of Miles, tears dropped from her chin like ragged raindrops onto his robed chest.

"I–I don't understand," Callie cried. "How could you? How could you do this to me? To us?"

Her voice was coming out in gasps, forcing its way out in between her wracking sobs. What kind of person—what kind of boyfriend—could do something like this? She loved him, wholeheartedly. She had even told him so. So, why did he do this?

"What's your favorite hor—" Miles began in his normal voice, before coughing. Blood dripped from his nose. "Isn't this what you've always wanted?"

"How could you!" Callie screamed. She plunged the knife into his chest, over and over. First an inch, then two, then three. Using the weight of her body to force it further.

"All this planning, all this time wasted," Callie sighed. There was anger in her voice now, no more tears. "I mean, Miles, they literally sell *the* mask at the store. And—and you show up in whatever the hell this thing is? Would it have killed you to do a little research and get the correct knife? I know you aren't a horror fan, but for me—for *me* you could have done better."

Callie pulled the knife out of Miles' chest. His blood pooled across the hardwood. She watched as it eked its way across the floor with macabre interest, her other hand tracing paths around the holes in his chest with bloody fingers, her t-shirt from mopping the tea earlier now soaked red in the corner.

"Oh, baby," Callie said, placing her head against his bleeding chest. "I mean, you even got the fucking line wrong."

Hours later, two Cemetery PD officers stood outside the Sanderson residence.

"Some crazy horror fanatic of a boyfriend decided to act out his favorite movie with his real-life girlfriend. Definitely not far-fetched for Cemetery. Don't you think?"

"Seems a little too perfect for me, honestly."

"Oh, come on," they said with a huff. "I gotta say, dressing up in a Halloween costume to hide your identity? Simple, but a hell of an idea."

DINNER DATE

Believe me when I tell you, I never once, in all the years of my life, thought I'd be going on a date with a man named *Vlad*. If a younger version of myself had told me that, I would have slapped myself silly.

But to be honest, he's so damn charming, it was too hard to say no. And his confidence? Through the roof. He looked me dead in the eyes and said, "you're going to dinner with me." After I came back to myself, came back from staring at his dreamy face, I realized it wasn't a question. It was a statement. More like a command.

Vlad is tall, devilishly handsome, and muscular. He is oddly pale, but he said he works nights, that he often spends the days tucked away sleeping. He has jet-black hair that always seems to be preternaturally perfect. And his wardrobe? It's as if he was plucked from out of a fashion magazine, every detail perfected like he has someone planning his every outfit. He's perfect, it's almost disgusting.

I wanted to argue and tell him off, to tell him no, I wasn't interested. But he's so put together. Almost *glamor*ous. I was kidding myself to think I could stop him. More than a tiny part of me wanted this, if I'm honest with myself. Which I'm often not...

When it comes to me, I'm far less than him. Less put together, less confident, less well dressed. And yes, honestly, even less tanned. I also work nights, not that he's asked, but it's one of the reasons that I have no problem with his lack of vitamin D. I had to rearrange my entire schedule to make tonight work, so his lack of interest really grates on my nerves.

Stood before the floor mirror in my bedroom, I feel nothing at all. As I so often do. I've got no fashion sense, no common sense even. Does this skirt match this top? Do I just wear jeans and a t-shirt? A dress? What about colors? And where the *hell* has my confidence gone? I know I'm far too old for this. But as I continue to stare into the mirror, there's *nothing* to look at: if there was, I'd stare back at my thin nose, pencil-straight black hair, my not-fit slim body.

So, why did Vlad ask out a woman like me? I'm not sure what it is he sees in me. What he wants with the likes of me.

I really don't know, but the ringing doorbell tells me I'm out of time. I look down at the silk dress I've just tried on. I give it one final colossal shrug, grab a scarf to cover my shoulders and my pocketbook, and head down to the door.

Vlad is wearing a suit that looks like every single stitch was made around the shape of his body. As if it was sewn right onto him. Do they give awards for things like that? Because whoever made it deserves one of some kind.

"May I come in?" he asks.

"Of course," I reply breathlessly, stunned at how good he looks. "Please, come in."

I stare down at my dress again, second-guessing every choice I've ever made in all my years. But Vlad simply leans in, placing a kiss on my cheek and handing me a red rose.

His lips are shockingly cold. To the point that the kiss startles me. Just how long was he standing outside?

"You look absolutely marvelous, darling," he says, his vaguely European accent becoming markedly more noticeable around the "rv" in marvelous.

The accent sends a shiver down my spine, in a way reminding me of home. It's one of the most attractive things about him. It draws you right in, hanging on every word that comes out of his mouth. And *darling*—who is this freaking guy?

"Should we get going?" I ask, hoping that my voice isn't quivering.

"Of course," he replies, taking my arm in his. "I've picked out one of the best restaurants in Cemetery."

After leading me to the car like a princess, or a child, he closes the door behind me. I watch as he works his way around the front. His stance is supremely relaxed, his movements butter-smooth. This is a person in their element. Why can't I feel that calm?

The car lights illuminate his face as he partially turns away from me, the look on his face all at once one that looks rather *monstrous*. His red-rimmed eyes reflecting the light look almost black in the stark beams. And not just the pupils.

My heart catches in my chest, but as he enters the driver's seat, his smile is back. Entirely normal again. The charm back in full display. Did I really even see anything?

The drive to the restaurant isn't a short one. We ride most of the way without speaking, the sound of some kind of classical symphony the only thing accompanying the silence. I can't count on one hand the number of people I know that drive around listening to classical music, because honestly, before today, it was a big fat zero.

It is kind of nice actually. There's a *hypnotic* quality to it, the plucking of string instruments soothing as the car lights carve a path through the foggy night.

Vlad parks the car in front of a restaurant called *Benucci's*. The sign is oversized and gaudy, speaking to its extravagance even though it is part of a strip mall. I take a few deep breaths, hoping that I won't make an absolute fool of myself inside. While Vlad's apparently a perfect human specimen, I am known for being a clumsy, if not even a messy, eater. I can just see it now: the buildup of his discomfort through the dinner, followed by him thrashing, fighting to escape the mess that I am.

That won't happen tonight though, right? *Please.*

After we're seated, Vlad smiles at me, his warmth working through me in a way I haven't felt in many years. I feel relaxation course through me. This is going to be okay. Totally fine.

"So," I begin, "do you have any family?"

"No," Vlad replies sharply, his tone uncharacteristic from what I've seen of him. He takes a breath, "Not for a long time anyway. I prefer to pick who I call family now. It's better that way for everyone. What about you?"

"Yes, my sisters," I start, the memory of them fresh and lovely. "But they're far away from here right now. They haven't been able to visit."

"Travel is still rather hectic at the moment, right?" Vlad offers, extending me a hand, the world post-Covid still stitching itself back together. "How many sisters do you have?"

"Just two younger ones. The three of us are very close," I reply, the corner of my lips turning up at the continued memories of my sisters. The years had been good to them, their beneficiary someone they could always *count* upon. "We spent a long time living together, but I wanted something new, somewhere fresh."

"Something new to *sink your teeth* into?" Vlad's lips purse in an overly suggestive way.

Something pulls at the back of my mind, making me want to lean forward and *devour* him without warning. Without thinking, without consent.

I'm saved from *eternal* embarrassment by the waitstaff. The man asks if we have had a chance to look at the drink menu yet. Vlad automatically orders for us both. Wine. The redder the better as far as I'm concerned.

The smile he follows up with is intoxicating. I feel myself drawn to him all over again.

As the waiter heads back toward our table, a tray with a bottle of wine and two glasses before him, a man from behind the bar steps out, cutting in front of him. I can see the waiter is looking back to check on another table, causing the two to crash into one another. The follow-up is the resounding smash of glasses and wine on the tiled floor.

The waiter bends down immediately, removing the tea towel from the front of his apron to soak up as much of the wine as possible. He mops it up as best he can with the small towel. With a sharp intake of breath, he yanks his hand back, a shard of glass sticking out of his thumb.

Vlad jumps up from his seat, his eyes red-rimmed and glaring, a *hungry* look on his face. He kneels before the man, removing the shard of glass from his finger, and placing pressure on the small cut.

After a minute, he removes his hand, the pressure doing well to stem the flow of blood.

As Vlad returns to the table, I think I catch him licking the waiter's *blood* from his finger, but I can't be sure. My pulse quickens as he smiles at me. "I just hate to see red wine wasted," he says with a big smile.

I take him in before me. Even after all that bending to help the waiter, he doesn't even look ruffled. I can't make out any creases in his suit; his hair is still perfect. As I stare deeply into his eyes, the only thing that strikes me as remotely different is a slight uptick in the *pulse* in his neck.

Yes. The scene caused by the waiter has certainly *awoken* a hunger in me. "Shall we order?" I ask.

"But of course." Vlad motions for the waiter, now finished cleaning. He strides over, pad in his hand at the ready. "I will take the *Spaghetti aglio e olio*, please. And for you, my Verona?"

"Wait, with—with *garlic*?" My face pales, "Fu—"

CAN YOU TURN IT DOWN

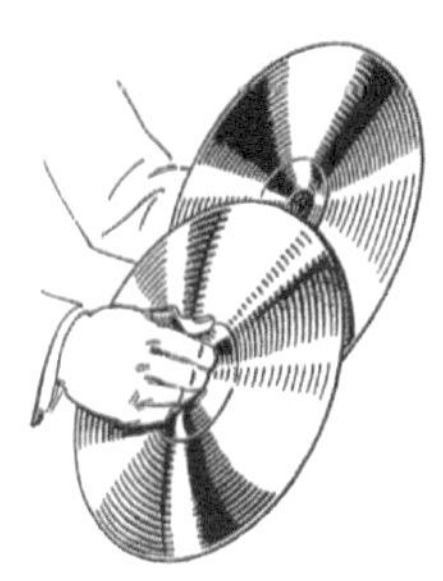

"Mom, it's been over a week already, come on!" Ashley pleads. Her fingers are crossed, but she isn't holding her breath.

"You were grounded for a month," Ashley's mother, Debbie replies. She shakes her head at her daughter, exasperated. She holds up her hands to ward off any arguing. "No, *no* Ashley, I don't want to hear it! It's a full month and that's final."

Angry tears well up in Ashley's eyes as she stares daggers at her mother.

Truth be told, she *had* been in the car with her friends. Her very young teenage friends. There had also been another much older *boy* driving the car. All in all, she knew she was breaking a cardinal rule, the punishment itself not surprising. But she had been on her best behavior for over a week, so wasn't this bordering on the ridiculous?

"This place is like a fucking prison!" Ashley yells as she runs to her room crying.

Debbie takes a deep breath, figuring it's better to let it go for now. Ashley knew she wasn't allowed to curse, just like she knew she was forbidden from being in the car with friends, but more fighting now would be imprudent.

The following afternoon, Ashley is in a far better mood. Although she's still grounded, it's not like her room is all that bad. It's small, but she's made the best of it.

To the left of the door is a desk, the shelves above it filled with stuffed animals she feels too old for but can't seem to part with. Her bed is directly across from it, just a small chair between the two. She loves the bed pressed directly against the wall, the lack of space allowing for her to recline while still resting her back against the wall itself. A *bright pink* wall that is. Her favorite color.

She doesn't have a TV but knows her mother wouldn't allow her to use it right now anyway.

She leans back with a pillow between her and the wall, a heavily used paperback in hand. Her current favorite is the *Sweep* series by Cate Tiernan. She's already halfway through a reread of the first book. There's just something so good about first person coming-of-age struggles that's hitting her so hard lately. Ashley might not be struggling with burgeoning witchcraft abilities like the main character of the story, but she is trapped in a way. Her own witch trial. And just for taking a car ride.

Her friends hadn't even done anything wrong. No speeding. No alcohol or drugs. No sexual activity, which weirdly seemed to be her mother's biggest fear. They went to the new Taco Bell in town. That's it. Not to mention it was because her mom *wouldn't* take them herself. Wow…when she thought about it, this was actually her mother's fault. Ashley would bring that up during their next fight, perfect fuel for later.

She didn't like being difficult. Truly she loved her mother, her life. So why did her mother like being so difficult?

Ashley's chin slowly droops toward her chest, dozing off while thinking how she would win their next bout.

Ashley awakes in a pool of her own drool.

"Come on, Ashley," Debbie says, shaking her daughter's shoulder. "Time to wake up."

Ashley shakes herself, wiping her mouth dry with the sleeve of her shirt before rolling over. "Is it my exercise time in the yard, warden?"

"Knock it off, Ashley, you're grounded because of your own decisions."

"Mom, you know, I've been thinking it over," Ashley begins, rubbing the sleep from her eyes. "And if you hadn't—"

"No, that's enough already, Ashley. I don't want to hear it. And I'm already late."

Ashley finally looks at her mother. She's in a navy dress, patterned in flowers in alternating pink, purple, and blues. Her makeup is also done, which is something Ashley hasn't seen in a long time.

"Wait, where are you going?"

"Your father is taking me to dinner," Debbie says, a smile crossing her face. "He said it was a date."

"Although mildly disgusted, it's unfair I'm trapped here while you're off gallivanting on a date with Dad."

"Yes, your father, *my husband*, the man that sleeps right down the hall?"

"Yeah, that's part of what makes the idea so gross, Mom."

Debbie scoffs, as if the thought is ridiculous, but her face says otherwise. She's hurt by the comment. "*Regardless*, your sister will be home to ensure you don't try running off. If you need anything, she'll be here to keep an eye on you. She's on her way home now."

"God, Mom, I'm not a freaking baby!"

"You're in enough trouble as it is, remember that." Debbie looks at her watch, shaking her head. "Look, I really am late."

Taking in the tear-streaked face of her daughter, Debbie sighs, defeated. "If you behave, then maybe we can discuss the terms of your grounding. I don't want to be the bad guy, but you need to know that when you're told no, it means *no*, okay?" She plants a quick kiss on her daughter's temple before shuffling out of the room, only sticking her head back in momentarily to utter "behave" before going.

IN ASHLEY'S INTERMINABLE BOREDOM, she peruses all the magazines in the house, even the ones in her dad's desk that she's sure she isn't supposed to see. Now that she has, she really wishes she hadn't. She wants to bleach her eyes instead.

Ashley ploughs through a bag of chips, a bowl of ice cream, three cheese sticks, and a soda. She doesn't want any of it, but without her parents home, she's able to break out of her cell for a bit. It feels too much like freedom to flounder an opportunity like that.

Ashley tries her hardest to stay in her room. She wants to get ungrounded more than anything, but then she remembers her mom said her sister was coming to make sure she didn't "try running off." She's positive that hadn't meant to the couch.

With a stomachache looming, Ashley stands in front of the windows that take up most of the wall in the living room. She moves the blinds and looks out toward the front yard. Their house is not on a road that has streetlights, so she can see about as far as the end of the porch, then everything else gets awfully hazy.

She stands there, watching, for probably half an hour. Just zoning out as her eyes randomly take in the passing of a car or the flicker of something out of the corner of her eye.

Then Ashley gasps, jumping, as a face moves out from the darkness. She drops the blinds, grabbing her chest and taking deep breaths.

As her heart rate settles, she peels the blinds back from the window again. There's nothing there. Just the darkness. *What in the world?*

She leans against the wall and laughs. She stared into the darkness for too long, too penned up. That's all. She's never seen the movie *Cabin Fever* due to her mother helicoptering, but she's certainly heard the term used by others. That's all it is. Just too cooped up thanks to her mother giving her twenty-five to life.

A creaking from downstairs makes her jump again. She curses herself for getting so nervy for no reason. Downstairs is where her sister's room is; her mother told her she would be here. Her not coming to say "hi" isn't all that surprising.

She and Kelly have been feuding lately. Kelly's older, already out of high school, and therefore treats the house like a hotel. Coming and going as she pleases. If Ashley's honest, she's not even angry, she's jealous. Why isn't their mother all over Kelly the same way she is Ashley? In a bad fight of theirs, Ashley had gone so far as to say it was because their mother had already given up on Kelly. Writing her off as lost. Kelly had cried right in front of her, but she'd been too mad to care.

The gap between them has widened since then.

Back in her bedroom, Ashley does her best to stay entertained. She listens to her CD player, a mix of songs that has frankly way too much Savage Garden. She gets into the rhythm of the songs, anyway, listening to the mix twice over before remembering that it's Kelly who showed them to her. She promptly shuts the player off, staring.

Even her music taste is making her feel trapped.

Ashley imagines her friends out having a blast. The time of their lives. Stopping for food at the Cemetery Diner, or seeing something without her at Cemetery Cinema, or just cruising to music. Driving around to wherever they want. Driving around with a specific *boy*. She could so easily get picked up. Her parents and Kelly would seriously never know.

Her chances of a "get out of jail free" card would probably go up in hellfire, though.

Her mind wanders while trying to read again, and for the most part she lets it. Every few pages she has to stop herself to reread entire paragraphs. Whenever her daydreaming gets dangerously close to sleep, she shakes herself and hops off the bed. Her bed is too familiar a hangout. The touch of the comforter makes her consider climbing beneath it every time.

There isn't really a reason to stay awake. However, part of her is hoping her parents will come home in good moods. The kind that involves a lot of laughing and a decent amount of alcohol. She doesn't know exactly what she'll spring on them, but figures there's a few hours to plan it out. *Let me out of this cage* runs through her head over and over.

A series of loud bangs startles her out of her mischief-making. Scheming pops from her mind like smoke. She looks around the room, wondering what's fallen, when she hears it again. Her attention snaps to the heating vent under her desk. It's the only direct shaft in the entire house. It runs from Ashely's room on the top floor directly to the furnace in the basement. It means that her room is always the coldest in the summer, hottest in the winter, and the loudest whenever someone is down there. Like Kelly. Her bedroom is the only furnished section built into the foundation. Ashley used to feel soothed by that connection, knowing that she was hearing Kelly made her feel safe. Like her sister could also hear her too if she was ever in need.

Now, Ashley is just pissed off. Whatever Kelly is doing sounds like a ten-piece band setting up their instruments. Is she rearranging her room? Is she using the dryer to spin a handful of nuts and bolts around? Ashley can't think of a single reason for Kelly to be so loud.

Then the noise stops. As if Ashley's room has gone from a carnival to being in a vacuum. A complete absence of sound. The longer the silence goes on, the stranger she feels about it. She feels confident she hasn't imagined it, but with it stopping so suddenly like that—could she have?

She sits down, staring at the wall and waiting to see if the noise will return. She looks blankly at a rough patch of paint, eyes settling on a bump in the pink. Paying more attention to what she's hearing than what she's seeing, the paint dances kaleidoscopically before her eyes. It seems to come alive the longer she sits. The longer she waits, listening. It's one of the strangest experiences she's ever had, allowing herself to zone out like this. It makes her dizzy, a little nauseous, and maybe even a little anxious.

What is she waiting for? Is she hoping to hear it again so she knows with certainty she isn't going crazy?

The silence rings out in her ears. A cacophony of non-sound, the clangor of lack thereof.

Her mother couldn't possibly keep her grounded longer if she's losing her mind, right? If she plunges into madness the responsibility will solely lie with her.

That's how Ashley sees it at least. She stays put.

Half an hour passes by in a flash, all while Ashley strains to hear something. She doesn't. She feels her anxiety rising as she stares at the bump on her wall. Blood pumps through her ears, pounding in a cadence that starts to feel and sound more and more like actual noise.

Is she sweating? She rubs her palms along her pajama pants, drying them. She rocks on the edge of the bed, no longer able to contain her anxiety. Is this a panic attack? Her chest hurts, constricting in a way she's never felt before.

Then she hears them.

Faint, only mildly registering as sound. It comes through the vent in altering tones. *Is that voices*? *Who the hell did Kelly bring over—Mom's going to flip*!

Then it gets louder.

"I don't know Gerry; they haven't accepted us yet. What would make them change?" the higher-pitched of the two voices asks.

"We have been together for over two years. Something's gonna have to give, honey."The second voice is deeper, decidedly male. The first voice is fainter, coming through the vent a bit distorted. Could that really be Kelly?

Has she been avoiding home because of some unapproved relationship with someone named Gerry? Why the hell didn't she tell me!

Ashley wracks her brain, trying her hardest to remember anyone in Kelly's life named Gerry. She comes up blank. So, who the hell is it?

"Mary Ann, listen to me. I love you, and I don't care what your two-timing father says about it. This is our life we're talking about. What we could have together. Not some time with your father who doesn't give a wink about you!"

The sound of faint sobbing echoes through the vent. Ashley sits bone stiff. Mary Ann and Gerry? Two-timing father? Who are these people?

The sobbing reaches a crescendo, peaking as if the person crying has nothing left to give. Ashley comes to her senses, raising herself from the bed, fighting through the panic.

Her hand lands firm against the door handle. The second she gives the handle a twist, the noise stops. Again. The vacuum is back with absolute silence.

The house doesn't shift or creak. The wind doesn't whistle past the house. No cars honk in the night. Everything is still. Again, she has the nagging feeling that she's imagined it.

She paces the small space, palms still sweating profusely. She's much too shaken to leave her room. The panic and fright claw their way up her neck; her stomach turns in waves of nausea and pain. Her insides feels as if something has crawled inside of her and dug around. All because she decided to get some fast food with friends. And for what? A tear runs down her face as she thinks about how it wasn't even all that good. Her rebellious teen moment wasted on nothing at all.

The overwhelming feeling of being trapped wedges its way into her like a heavy stone. Ashley throws herself onto the bed, clawing her way under the covers, convinced that she just needs to wait for her parents to get home. If she can wait until then, everything will be fine.

There are no noises coming from downstairs. There are no noises coming from downstairs. There are no noises coming from downstairs. There are no noises coming from downstairs.

Ashley chants it like a mantra until she falls into fitful sleep.

SHE WAKES WITH A start, the feeling of dread meeting her the second her brain switches back on. She rolls onto her back. Allowing herself to fully awaken.

The sound of music wafts its way through the vent. Syncopated rhythms pulse and lilt while a trumpet bleats over it all. It must have been what woke her. It's something she's never heard before, and it's blaring. She thinks of ska—but that feels off—jazz? With the space growing between her and Kelly, she isn't surprised she has no idea what she likes to listen to anymore.

Anger replaces the feeling of dread. She's stuck here at home, and her sister—who's honestly not even that much older than her—has been called home to babysit her like some corrections officer. Her sister, who doesn't even like being around her anymore, is here to ensure that no fun is had. Nor freedom. Meanwhile, that same sister blasts shitty music through the downstairs vent, ensuring that Ashley can't relax. Can't even sleep her way through imprisonment.

All while her parents are out on a date no less! Her mother dangling freedom before her like a lamb chop to a starving bear.

This has to stop. It's messed up. So fucking *unfair*. It's an injustice served.

Ashley leaps from the bed, grabbing the house phone off the desk and jumping back under the covers. She dials Kelly's cellphone. Nothing. Again. Dial tone, ringing, nothing.

"Answer your phone," Ashley shouts in frustration. "Come on, come on," she mumbles under her breath as she dials again.

It's as if every time she dials Kelly's phone, the music raises in volume. The sound of keys blare up the vent as if a grand piano has been dragged into the basement, all while the trumpet bleats. By the fourth or fifth time, it's as if a live band is in the bedroom with her. Deafening. She doesn't think time apart would be enough to change Kelly's music taste so drastically. It takes her a long time to realize she's crying hysterically. *Come on, come on, come on. What the* hell *is going on!*

Finally, on her tenth attempt, on the final ring, Kelly answers. "Why are you blasting your music so loud? Why are you being so mean to me? You really couldn't even say hi?"

"Woah, woah, slow down Ashley. Calm down, please. What the hell are you talking about?"

Ashley takes a deep breath, hiccupping while she tries to center herself. She's at an eleven out of ten. She needs to come down to an eight to speak clearly. All while the music blares.

It's just music, isn't it? Annoying, yes. Harmful, no.

"Can you turn it down?" she asks.

"Turn it down? What are you talking about Ashley?"

"The music! Come on, stop messing with me. It's bad enough being cooped up in the house. For Christ's sake can you turn the music down at least?"

"Ashley, that's not funny. I'm not home yet. I got caught up at work. That's why I didn't answer the first few times. I'm walking to my car now."

It does sounds like she's outside and moving. But that would mean Kelly really isn't home. That Ashley is in the house by herself...

"You're really not here?"

"No, Ashley, I'm not."

Tears carve salty streaks down Ashley's face as the music grows ever louder. She tries to ask Kelly to hurry, but she's already dropped the phone. Maybe she really did see a face outside earlier. Hours ago, when she could have called the police, when she could have run.

The music is painful, as if each cymbal crash is next to her ear. Maybe, if she can just reach the door, the sound will cut off like before. If she can just power through the paralytic fear and move.

With each step the sounds grow louder, coming alive. They undulate violently, threatening to perforate her eardrums. As she nears the door, to break free from her imprisonment, one thing becomes clear...she was never alone in here.

SÉANCE

I OPENED THE FRONT door, smile plastered on my face, and grabbed my cousin up in a giant bear hug. It had been too long, and Emilio was showing more changes than expected. At seventeen, he was taller, broader, and had stubble along his jaw. He was becoming a man. A miniature man, but still. He looked clean cut; his Nike t-shirt and slim-fit jeans were a nice sight. I was still taller than him, more filled out, but it was surprising how fast he was catching up.

Since his father's death, I had taken it upon myself to fill in. To be the man in his life. An example. Our busy lives at work and school respectively were just about the only things that used to keep us apart. But as he grew older, he found a life of his own, and I had to learn to accept that space between us. It made me cherish our times together that much more.

Behind Emilio, his friend Sammy looked less pleased to see me. Sammy was heavyset, looking particularly big in his undersized North Face Steep Tech. His sweatpants were rounded out with a pair of Addidas slides. I silently thanked God he was wearing socks. Sammy had been Emilio's hanger-on since they were kids. Now that they were nearing adulthood, the friendship seemed more one-sided than ever. I was honestly shocked my cousin had brought him. Our private conversations were less than favorable in terms of Sammy in recent years.

"Hey, Trey," my cousin said, hugging me back. "How you been?"

"Good, man, good. Same as ever, really. How's my favorite tía?"

"Mom's good, cuz. Working a lot and taking it out on me, but what else is new?" Emilio grabbed my shoulders firmly, giving them a good shake. "She's good though."

"Glad to hear it. And what's up with you, Sammy?"

Sammy took my hand up in a sweaty, gross handshake. "You're looking real old, man," Sammy said with a humorless laugh.

"Yeah, thanks. Just you guys wait until you reach twenty-five, alright?" I said back with a laugh, choosing to ignore the jab.

Emilio gave Sammy the kind of look that said "watch your damn mouth, man" without speaking a word. He had that way about him, was good at reading my nonverbal cues. The two friends never seemed to fight amongst themselves, but Emilio would go to bat for me before letting me smack the teen.

I stepped back and let them both inside instead. They headed toward the kitchen island of my apartment as I locked the door behind them. The back of my programmed brain set alarms off at them walking around with their shoes on—my mother would smack me upside the head if she knew—but I ignored it.

Emilio popped the refrigerator, grabbing three beers and tossing one to Sammy. I wasn't one for speaking out against underage drinking. I did it and turned out just fine. And what better place to have a beer than safely with your older cousin? Neither of them drove anyway. I'd make them stay later and eat something before letting them go either way.

Sammy popped on the TV, placing the underside of his slides right on the edge of my antique oak coffee table. I opened my mouth to light him up, then I caught how badly the Knicks were getting stomped and got angry about that instead.

"This isn't the team I remember anymore," I said, fury bleeding into my tone.

"Nah, it just hurt less when you were younger." Sammy laughed around his beer and Emilio joined him.

I reluctantly allowed the blow to land. Perhaps he's not wrong. I cracked open my own beer instead of answering, taking a solid gulp. The carbonation caught in my nose, and I quickly blinked it away to keep my eyes from tearing. When I looked up, Emilio was watching me out of the corner of his eye.

"So, how's old Cemetery High treating you two, still on track to graduate?" I asked.

"Yeah, Trey, with honors. That's not the kind of thing you just lose."

"No, I guess not. Tía Rosalie would get after your ass, too." I paused to take another sip. "I'm just surprised you're able to get Sammy to class is all."

Sammy's dark complexion darkened further in anger. He knew I was referring to the year he was left behind for never showing up, choosing to skip school and hangout with other friends while Emilio hustled to make something of himself. It was another thing that set them so far apart. My cousin swore that Sammy was brilliant, just unenthused with the banality of schoolwork. Personally, it was something I would have believed only if my eyes could see it.

It might have been due to the plummeting opinion I'd had of him over the years due to his bloodsucking attachment to Emilio and his talents, but I'd sooner believe he was as smart as the slides attached to his feet. Not that I was any kind of homerun in school either, but I was scraping by now, setting aside little by little.

Not that either of them cared about something like that. They couldn't. They weren't plunged into the deep, cold waters of reality yet. I'd let them stay away a while longer.

We ordered buffalo wings, drinking our way through several more beers, and continued to watch as the Knicks gave the game away. Emilio began to meld with the couch cushions, allowing his full belly and drunken mind to wander and fade out. I watched as the beer between his legs became less and less supervised, his head bobbing.

Soon, Sammy became fidgety. When I saw him actively refreshing his Instagram feed, I knew he was about to start complaining. Truth is, I had a plan for tonight. I had it all mapped out already. Sammy was the first hiccup, but I could work it into a benefit. I couldn't allow there to be a second one.

For months, I had been spending time at this shop. It was one of those hippie places from another era that always smelled like incense and sweat, but I felt as if something kept drawing me there. It wasn't causing any harm, or more importantly costing any money. Frankly I was enamored.

The storefront was small, unremarkable, and bordering on invisibility. It read "Nathan's Apothecary" in barely lit lettering, the neon long past its heyday. Nathan, the store's owner and sole employee, was a shockingly gangly white guy with dreadlocks. And, more importantly, the exact kind of person I expected to run a shop like that.

I don't recall what first made me enter, and I guess it doesn't really matter anymore. On Thursday nights after work, I found myself walking through shelves of dusty books. The rows of moldy spines and water-damaged pages made me think of hidden societies and ancient locations. Divination, tea-leaf readings, and *im*practical remedies were foreign to me, but something about how aged they were spoke to me on a primal level. For weeks Nathan and I exchanged random eye contact, both looking away whenever we felt caught. I didn't know why I kept going back, and I thought he had a problem with me never spending money.

But in the weeks that followed, we finally spoke. I don't recall what started it, but he was a treasure trove of anecdotes. I became even more curious about the place. We'd spent hours on end talking about things both past and present. When we became comfortable together, he told me he felt my connection to the place, knew I'd keep coming back. I recall being confused by what he meant.

Nathan spoke at length about how I was the perfect candidate for performing a séance, that I had a connection to the other side. A sentence that should be laughable to say, but somehow it felt right. He'd earned my trust, so I believed him.

"You know what," Nathan had said, "I'm going to get together some items for you to give it a try."

"Why?" I'd said. I couldn't think of anything else to say, and I followed it with a cough. It was the first time he had ever offered me anything, and though moments before I felt trust, this had felt out of place.

"Why? Because this is why you've been coming here all along!" Nathan smiled. For a moment it seemed genuine. But as he held it for longer, it took on an almost clownish quality in its wideness. Like he was showing too many teeth. I didn't like it.

Being at a loss for words had never been a problem for us. We had become fast friends—albeit the location was a bit weird—but now I didn't know what to do.

Nathan loaded a box with everything he said I would need and told me it was at no cost. I didn't have the extra cash to argue, but I hadn't exactly asked for it either. I accepted, though numbly, taking the box from him and making my excuses to leave.

Even then, I'd left the box in the trunk of my car for weeks. Probably not the best plan, as the box included candles, but I had no clue what to do with it. Eventually, the curiosity got to me, and I found myself researching and watching videos online late into the night. Things like mediumship grabbed my attention right away. The idea that I could possibly funnel messages from the other side, either consciously or subconsciously, was such a spooky and cool idea. When it came to the tools others used, like Ouija boards, I was far less enthused. The idea of opening something up for a possible demonic presence seemed far-fetched, but not impossible. If I was going to entertain the idea at all, that meant I had to buy fully into it, right?

Sammy slid his cellphone back into his pocket for the fifteenth time. As he opened his mouth to talk, I knew my plan was solidified.

"I'm bored as shit, man. What are we doing?" Sammy leaned over and smacked Emilio on the shoulder. He started to full attention with a groan.

"What do you mean, 'What are we doing?' We're here to hang out with Trey for the night. Drinking beers, eating wings, and watching basketball. What the hell else would you do?" Emilio was either annoyed at being woken up, or angry with Sammy for being problematic.

"I don't know, play video games?"

"Why would we sit and play 2K when a *real* basketball game is live on TV right now?" Emilio rolled his eyes.

"Man, I don't know. It's more entertaining when you're the one doing it." Sammy wasn't about to let it go.

"Just shut up, man." Emilio finished his latest beer and stood up to go into the kitchen. "I was all happy tipsy and now you're being annoying for no reason."

Sammy's features darkened again, but he didn't reply in anger. "Okay, I'm sorry. Was just saying I'm bored."

Emilio put his empty can in the recycling bin under the sink, then opened the fridge to grab another round. I noticed his movements were a little off. He knocked over one of the beers before he could remove it from the fridge. It hit the kitchen floor with a *crack*, beer hissing out of whatever hole had been punctured and leaking all over the scuffed, light-brown linoleum tiling. He was past tipsy by my reckoning, and I wondered if that would make him pliable or touchy for this next part.

Emilio stood shakily, chagrined, his cheeks reddening deeper than the flush of alcohol. "Sorry, Trey. I guess I'm a little drunker—"

"Yo, it's cool. But I know what we can do if you're both bored."

Emilio straightened up, face uncertain, but I thought he was leaning toward taking whatever was on offer to avoid further embarrassment. He grabbed a handful of paper towels to give himself time to think it over.

I wondered what he was thinking. Why the hesitation? "Come on, Emilio, it'll be fun. It'll take your mind off dirtying my kitchen floor..."

Why was he being that way, why the uncertainty? And why so embarrassed about a single beer? You don't cry over spilled beer.

Emilio made direct eye contact and nodded. "I'm in, what's up?"

"A séance."

"The fuck did you just say?" Sammy chimed in.

"I said, we're going to do a séance." I thought better of it. "Well, we're going to *try* to do a séance."

"We don't know the first thing about séances. Why would we even want to attempt one?" Sammy questioned.

"I've been reading up on it, okay? I have all the stuff we need. I just want to give it a shot. And—and if it doesn't work, fuck it, we'll play 2K for the rest of the night." Emilio opened his mouth to reply, but I cut him off. "Hey, you already said you were in!"

"Okay, you're tempting me with talks of 2K, but *why* are we trying to do a séance?" Sammy asked.

"This guy, Nathan, told me he thinks I've got some kind of connection to the other side. That I can act as the conduit or some shit for a séance. He gave me this whole box of junk for free and told me to try. I thought he was nuts, but maybe it's something from our family—some ancestral brujo shit...why not give it a go?" I could tell my reasoning was falling on deaf ears. I tried giving them the full backstory behind my trips to the Apothecary. Sammy wasn't the least bit interested, and Emilio was still standing there with his mouth half open. "Emilio—Em, if this works, we could contact your dad. We could get answers about what really happened. This can work."

I wanted to sound sure, but I wasn't positive I did. Honestly, I wasn't. I couldn't be. But I really wanted to give this a try.

"Okay." Emilio's voice was small, uncertain—almost child-like.

"For fuck's sake," Sammy said.

I jumped into action. Clearing off the beer and wing detritus from the coffee table, I placed the couch cushions around it. We'd have to be seated close enough to touch hands. I thought about the kitchen island, but that would leave one of us awkwardly leaning over the sink. Criss-cross style around the coffee table would be best.

I set about placing and lighting the candles, the matches' sulfuric scent filling the living room. The smell reminded me of my childhood, our beat-up gas stove's auto-lighter long dead, the memory of my mom's authentic pozole and tamales bringing a warmth to the moment. I'd have to remember to call her soon.

I finished off with a single candle in the center of the table, the candle I'd call upon the spirit with.

I motioned for Sammy and Emilio to get on the cushions until they finally listened. I ran to the kitchen, ripping through cabinets until I found what I was looking for. I popped the lid and sprinkled a circle of salt around the three of us. Then, finally, I sat down.

"Did the weird *wook* dude tell you to do that with the salt?" Emilio asked.

"Uh, no," I replied. A bit embarrassed, I said, "I actually got that from *Hocus Pocus*."

"The shitty witch movie?" Sammy interjected.

"Woah..." I said sternly, "we do not have time to go into that right now. Let's start."

"What do we do?" Emilio asked. He looked a little shaky and his voice slurred at the end. I figured it was just the idea of reaching out to his dad. Or all the beer.

"We all have to picture your father as clearly as possible. What he meant to us, who he was in our eyes, and how we simply wish to make contact. Nothing else. Let's give that a shot before I start."

We sat in silence, Emilio's head turned up in concentration. Now that it was go-time he had gotten serious. Sammy had his eyes closed and was mumbling. I hoped it was about memories of Tío Eddy, but I had my doubts.

Finally, I closed my eyes too. I thought of tío and the night of the accident. Tía Rosalie had called me hysterical. "Where is Emilio? You have to go find him right now!" she had yelled. I hadn't known where to start, but I grabbed my keys and left. When I had found Emilio, he was riding his bike around town with some friends. I made up an excuse to get him in the car, I don't even remember what it was. When we arrived at the hospital, the way Emilio clung to me was something I'll never forget until the day I die. The despair, the pain, the brokenness in his eyes. That's what tío meant to me. To us. Eddy was everything to this family. And then he was just *gone*.

"Alright, guys, I think we're ready to start. Give me your hands," I said.

"I'm not holding your hands like some—"

Emilio cut Sammy off, swatting his arm hard. Sammy winced, rubbing the smarting arm and whispering obscenities.

Sammy leaned in for my outstretched hand, taking Emilio's in his other. Clearly my cousin had decided to give this a real shot.

I took a deep breath to center myself. This was it. This was the end to my weeks-long anticipation. I couldn't avoid the possibilities any longer. I had to try.

I imagined myself opening. Whether it be my soul, my being, or like a third eye or something, I had no idea. I never once stopped to think about what I could be inviting in.

Through steady breathing, I kept my focus on the center candle, mesmerized by its gyrations and susurrations. The dancing, flickering light around the polished table. The all-too distracting way you could be lulled by its movements. It almost made me feel lax, safe even. It was just me and the candle.

"Now it's time to begin. Sammy, Emilio, remember that as soon as we start, we can't stop. Once I invite the spirit of your father here, we cannot break the circle. Okay? Our hands stay together no matter what."

"No matter what," the two parroted.

I tightened my grip on their hands to add weight to the statement. I really was out of time, of options.

With a rasping inhale, I invited him in.

"Tío Eddy, if you're out there, we invite you into our circle. If you're out there, we want to share our time with you. If you're out there, please reach out for us."

Sammy stared at the center candle, fully absorbed but not necessarily believing. Emilio, on the other hand, sounded as if he might have been hyperventilating.

It *was* his father after all.

"Tio Eduardo, if you're there just beyond the wall, please reach for us. We three invite you in! Eduardo Guerra, if you're there beyond the veil, we are reaching for you. Please come into our circle."

A moment passed and then another. I didn't feel any different, but the air in the living room had taken on a chill. Not enough to see our breath, but cold enough to make me wonder if I'd left the bedroom window open again.

"Eddy, if you're here with us, please move the candle's flame to the left. Please manipulate the fire to let us know you've made it."

We watched the candle in a vacuum of silence, our breaths held.

After a couple of minutes, Sammy began to stir. Nothing had happened. I had felt so damn certain it would have.

"Uh, it's not working, Trey," Emilio said. He looked sad, as if he really had hoped it would.

"Yeah, I think someone promised me 2K?" Sammy said.

"No! Don't break the circle," I yelled at them, tightening on their hands. "What did I tell you? You can't break the circle while the invite is open. Let's—let's try it again, Em. If I'm some kind of conduit, maybe you are too? We are cousins. Ask if your dad is here, but let's do it together."

Emilio took in the room. The dimmed lights, the flickering candles, the circle of salt. Maybe it hadn't truly felt real up until that point, but when he looked at me, I saw a steeliness to his glare. "I'm ready."

Together we called upon Eddy. I called for my tío and he called for his father. It felt as if Emilio was adding strength to whatever it was we were pulling upon. Not quite opening a floodgate, but I felt more of a flow than before.

The flame bent to the left at a ninety-degree angle. There was nothing to dispute. Flames were an ever-moving entity, but they did *not* bend at exact angles.

Our exclamations of "Tío" and "Dad" filled the air at the same time. Both of us sounded breathy in disbelief. We'd done it.

We'd *done* it.

The temperature in the room had settled into a decided cold, the carbon dioxide leaving our lungs in cloudy puffs. No open window could affect the temperature that much.

"Dad, can you talk to us? What happened the night of your accident?" Emilio blurted, the words leaving him all in a rush.

The flame of the candle continued to flicker and bend, but no vocal answer followed.

"Shit, should you have bought a *wee-jah* board for this or something?" Sammy asked.

"*Ouija* boards are known to invite in more evil than good. I wasn't about to mess with something like that," I said.

"So how the hell do we communicate with him now that he's here?" Sammy replied.

"We use the candle. Ask him to bend it. We'll have to go with yes or no answers, but that should work."

"If you're actually here with us, Dad, please bend the candle again," Emilio said.

The flame bent unnaturally.

The goosebumps up and down Emilio's arms were visible from across the table.

"Was the crash the night you died your fault? Bend the flame to the left for yes and right for no."

"Jesus, Sammy, what the fuck?" I snapped at him.

"You said we were getting answers about that night. You don't think that's a valid question?" Sammy said in defense.

Before I could answer, the flame bent to the right for "no." So the accident that night hadn't been caused by Eddy. The relief was evident, Emilio's shoulders slumping in a release of tension.

"So some—someone else caused the crash that killed you. Do you know who did it?" Emilio asked.

"This isn't about some kind of weird revenge, Emilio. It was an accident," I warned.

"These assholes out here never pay attention for motorcycles. An accident was what it was labeled, but why didn't they wait at the scene?" Emilio rapid fired at my response.

"I don't know, Em, but that doesn't mean you go looking for troub—"

The flame bent left for "yes." Yes, Tío Eddy knew who had caused the crash. I wished I knew how to cut off our connection to him—this had been a bad idea. The information would only reignite Emilio's anger over his father's death. Not to mention we could only communicate through yes and no answers. Emilio's inability to get a spelled-out answer might only enrage him further. I had intended for this to be healing.

"Was it someone we know?" Emilio asked the cold room.

"Wait, why would it be someone we know?" Sammy questioned.

"Just a feeling."

The flame yet again bent to the left for "yes." Emilio sucked in a ragged breath that sounded painful.

"How can he convey who to us, Trey?"

"I don't know, Emilio. We're working with yes and no—or at best one-word answers. I don't see how he could convey a name," I answered.

"'Kay." I saw Emilio grinding his teeth in the flickering candlelight. He banged his knuckles on the table in anger, startling Sammy as he pulled his hand down hard with his. His glossy eyes scanned the room as he thought of a way to work it out. "Fine, okay. Let's start simple. Use us as a baseline."

"Tío, we're going to ask a few more complex questions. We'll figure out a way for you to answer, okay? Let's start simple again. Am I the person that caused your crash?"

The flame bent to the right for "no." I felt a sheen of sweat on my forehead despite the cold.

"Was it me, Dad?"

As soon as Emilio finished his question, the flame bent left for "yes." Over and over and over again. Flickering and flashing. With tears in his eyes, Emilio jumped back, Sammy and I just managing to hold his hands. The center candle's flame grew to over three feet, the heat blazing across the coffee table threateningly.

"DO NOT BREAK THE CIRCLE!" I gripped the boys' hands as hard as I could.

"How?" was all that Emilio could slur out. His voice squeaked and the tears in his eyes were dangerously close to falling.

The temperature dropped to subzero, our breath hanging before us in thickening clouds in the still air. The flame of the center candle slowly lowered back to normal. When it shrank back to original size, the candles surrounding the table snuffed out, the deepened darkness doing nothing to calm our erratic heart rates.

"What the fuck was that?" Sammy said.

"Uhh, I don't think that was Emilio's dad. What I felt was really dark, like overbearing, not the typical warmth of tio." My statement hung in the air like our clouds of breath. No one moved.

Emilio began to sob on his side of the table. His body shook violently and every part of me wanted to pull him to me. To console him and tell him this wasn't his fault, that none of it was. It hadn't been his father, so he couldn't believe a single word that'd been said. It was my fault this happened. But I couldn't break the circle yet.

"We rescind the offer to our circle, our table. We rescind our time with you. We rescind our open arms. You are no longer welcome here. Be gone!" With each sentence, with each rebuttal, my voice grew louder. Stronger. My control coming back. We hadn't broken the circle; the spirit, demon, or whatever it was, was at our mercy.

Ever so softly, the candle in the center of the table snuffed out. I didn't feel the entity leave, but as a first-time experience, I wasn't exactly sure I had felt them in general.

"Wow, that was actually nuts," Sammy said, scratching his thumb up and down the side of his nose.

"Emilio, you can't believe any of that, okay?"

Emilio just sniffled. His body hadn't fully caught up to the fact that it was over. He wiped his hand down his face, clearing away the tears and snot.

Wait—

Sammy *scratched* his nose. Emilio *wiped* his face. The circle was broken.

I had not told them it was okay to break the circle.

The flame in the center of the table shot back to life. It grew so large that its flickering end tickled the ceiling. The paint bubbled black.

"I didn't say we could break the fucking circle!" I yelped.

My voice was lost in a whirlwind of cold breath and salt rising from the floor. The wind picked up, swirling around us to create a globe of tornado-like winds. Pictures ripped from the walls, the nails previously holding them in place stripping from the studs. The PlayStation remotes from the TV stand whipped into the corners of the walls, smashing into millions of tiny pieces.

The salt around us created a protective barrier, zipping around in the winds but keeping us from the smashing debris that used to be my home décor. My cousin and his best friend tried to grab hands again, but the wind was too strong. Emilio tugged his hand back toward his chest, while Sammy was slowly losing the fight, his hand pulled behind his back with a sickening snap.

The two of them screamed for me, but I couldn't hear a word.

I had done this. This was all my fault. And I was powerless to stop it.

I tried to think of ways to banish an evil entity, but my mind had gone blank, numb. All the extensive research I had done was sucked out of my brain by the powers at play.

As I reached for my cousin's hand, one of the framed pictures from the wall carved a zigzagged cut through the layer of salt surrounding us. The barrier finally breached, all the broken bits and grit hit us like living room shrapnel.

Halfway across the table, our hands inched through the breakneck winds. A piece of controller sliced across the back of Emilio's hand. He gasped in pain, the blood flying upward in the gale. My reflexes told me to bring my hand back for protection. I fought the urge.

I reached with all my might for my little cousin. My desire, my desperate need, to protect him taking over. This was my idea, my fault. I had started it all. What did it matter if I got hurt? Emilio already was. I needed to save him. I screamed my anger, my worry, my defeat, into the air. I doubted if either of them could hear it, but I harnessed that scream, propelling my hand through.

As my fingers brushed against my cousin's hoodie, a flash of purple light popped into existence between him and Sammy. My hand bobbed up and down, the shoelace string of the hood bouncing off my middle fingernail as I pushed onward.

The purple light came to life. It cracked open, splitting into what looked like a million pieces of glass. A mosaic that shouldn't exist.

It all happened so fast. I didn't even have time to think. All the air in the room: the debris, the salt, the candles, and then my cousin Emilio and Sammy were sucked through that crackling purple *portal*.

With a *snap*, the portal disappeared, the air stilled, and all lay silent.

I breathed heavily, oxygen fighting its way to my air sacs to keep me going. I collapsed against the table in utter disbelief. I had just watched them disappear into thin air, as if they had never been there at all. None of this should have been possible.

What in God's name did I do?

I had to call the cops. I had to call my tía and tell her what happened. I had to call in nuns and priests. The fucking pope. We needed holy water and hellfire. We needed to get them back.

I needed to get them back.

Hours later, as some asshole officer crudely shoved me into the back of a police cruiser, I still didn't know what my first steps should be. The police had arrived and seen the state of the place. They saw the blood spatter on and around me, and when they couldn't find any obvious cuts, assumed the worst of me. It did look as if quite a struggle had happened. They must have assumed I'd given them some cock-and-bull story. My neighbors gave noise complaints, but no one believed it'd been wind. They only cared that I was alone, probably assuming I'd stashed a body somewhere. They wanted to take me in for questioning.

The temperature in my apartment hadn't returned to normal by the time they arrived, the chill a mind-numbing reminder of what I had caused. So when they asked me to come down to the station, I said yes and didn't put up any resistance.

Anything to get away from there.

KNIGHT OF THE LIVING DEAD

The wooded, dense area around Cemetery made it an obvious candidate for a *Renaissance Faire*. The land was purchased and then carved out in the perfect location to make fairgoers feel like Robin Hood-rangers, bandits, medieval knights, jousters, woodland elves, and whatever else they could imagine.

Each year the event grew until the need for parking was such that the committee had to purchase another lot of land to turn into a private area for visitors' cars. This additional space made their property so large that they turned to additional events for revenue.

With the fair being seasonal, the committee eventually landed on a fall event filled with blood and horrific scares. They would retrofit the established buildings into haunted houses, and add tents, blowups, and mazes in the fields.

Cemetery's *Scream Fest* became the second largest annual event.

Mitchell stood rocking against the desk in the administration building, the loose tunic of his knight costume catching on the edge. The lack of air conditioning was a real point of contention with the staff during the hot summer months, but Mitchell was completely unfazed. As the Manager of Events, he was meant to put on a brave face and bear it, and he was technically enduring it, however subconsciously—or perhaps unconsciously.

It had happened during the last week of the *Renaissance Faire*; Mitchell had stepped behind one of the partition walls to take a piss when some drunken idiot had attacked him from behind. With dick in hand, he was caught off guard, only one hand to defend himself. He was overpowered, bruised and scraped up, and the bastard had *bitten* him.

Mitchell did his best to clean himself up, dusting his crimson-colored tunic off and hoping he hadn't gotten piss on himself. Too busy to run to a hospital, he was low on options for the bite, finally settling for a bottle of vodka that the staff had stashed away. He screamed as the liquor burned across his bleeding arm, the teeth marks visible as the clear liquid replaced the red. Not wanting to be perceived as weak, he duct-taped a washcloth to his forearm and got back to work.

The rest of that first night he spent in silent agony, the rage fueling him to finish faster.

By the final evening of the fair, he had entirely changed in the few short days. He was pale and emaciated-looking, as if the weight had simply melted off his large frame. And he was always covered in a thick sheen of sweat. He promised those around him he was fine, but they gave him a wide berth.

The bite on his arm had turned a sickly yellow green, the smell of which reminded him that he should have seen a doctor. Instead, he continued his diet of alcohol and painkillers; he had a job to complete. Not that the end of summer really marked the end of work for him, as Mitchell also oversaw *Scream Fest*, but he could see the doctor during the couple weeks of prep.

But Mitchell hadn't seen a doctor. After that night, closing up the fair and saying goodbye to his staff, he had stumbled, blurry eyed and dizzy, into the administration building. Eager to grab the company phone to dial 911, Mitchell had instead tripped, smashing the front of his head against the desk.

When he had awoken—or *unwoken*—his brain fed him loose information to drag himself to his feet. He had been standing, swaying, and bumping into the office desk ever since. A thin layer of forehead was folded back on itself from where he had hit the desk. A family of flies landed on the festered wound and crawled over his white, vacant eyes.

The costume sword that hung from his hip clanked against the desk, the pommel quivering with a metallic ring.

The weight continued to drop from his body as the days spent in the administration office grew, his fat stores turning to liquid as his diseased body slowly ate away at itself. His costume tunic hung limp from his body, his unbathed skin emitting an unpleasant scent that spread throughout the space. The cloying, fetid air crowded the office like a miasma.

It smelled as if someone had *died*.

With the staff being so seasoned, the prep work was going off without a hitch. Therefore, no one had knocked for Mitchell in the past fortnight. To him it could have been minutes.

Creaking hinges off to the side drew a stir within the confines of Mitchell's foggy mind. He turned slowly with unpracticed steps. A man stepped back out through the door, gagging and emptying the contents of his stomach over the railing.

Coming back in, the man said, "Jesus, Mitchell, what the fuck happened? Are you alright?" He edged forward, eyes lined with worry. "Mitch, what happened to your eyes?"

As the man entered Mitchell's range, desiccated arms stretched forward, the once-infected bite turned a gritty black. The thin arms grasped their prize and drew it toward their goal. To feed. To fill. To gnaw.

The man, who was only trying to be helpful, was cut down in short order with a juicy crunch. Not even getting a chance to scream.

"Where the hell is Jeremy?"

"I got no idea, Donnie, he was supposed to grab Mitchell."

Donnie paced, irate. He wore a grey hoodie with a v-shape cut out of the collar, his heavyset neck still struggling to fit. He threw the crumpled hat from his hands onto the dirty ground, stomped it for good measure. "All we needed Mitch for was to give the final go-ahead for opening tonight. That little shit's probably run off."

"Sorry, Donnie. Jeremy did say something about quittin' again. Maybe he jetted?"

Donnie placed a cigarette into his mouth, giving himself a minute. "At least he waited until the actual work was done. But to run off right before we open the gates? He'll get what's coming to him."

Grabbing the walkie-talkie off his truck bed, Donnie called for a staff meeting in fifteen minutes. He tried to finish his cigarette in relative calmness, but an uneasy feeling had overtaken him, Jeremy's untimely exit overhanging like a suspicious cloud. One less set of eyes overseeing the crowds, one less set of hands to help. It's not like he could count on the crew in costume, their jobs were to scare the holiness out of the *Scream Fest* goers. He knew if there was one thing that would ruin the bit, it was them breaking character. So, he and Timmy would have to pick up the slack.

He closed his eyes, allowing the nicotine to seep through his worked muscles and stressed mind. He knew he shouldn't be feeling this way, but he had the creeps. What kind of an idiot gets the creeps at a haunted house event that they were *working*? A faint rustling, like feet dragging through tall grass, drew his attention.

Donnie opened his eyes and yelped. As he jumped in fright, he shoved out, knocking Timmy flat on his ass. "What the fuck are you still doing here?" he said through gasping breaths.

Timmy chuckled as he wiped mud from the ass of his jeans. "I wasn't trying to startle you, sorry—"

Timmy stared over Donnie's shoulder at a blur of motion behind the truck. The growing dark was upon them, and as they waited for the gates to open before launching the event lights, it was too dark to decipher what he'd seen. "Donnie, I think I just saw Mitchell, but I'm not sure. It looked like he was still dressed as a knight."

"He wasted his nitpicking time being off somewhere else. I'm not about to argue with someone still dressed like the *RenFaire* is going on...we gotta open."

Timmy continued staring at the spot he saw the blur. "Course I know that, Donnie. But we could use his help on the lines without Jeremy, no?"

Donnie nodded his head. "I'll do the opening meeting, you go grab Mitch's lazy ass and get him out here."

TIMMY FOLLOWED THE BLUR around the corner, the backside of the haunted house giftshop lined with porta johns. The fair had its own set of restrooms, but with the heightened excitement and fear going around, bowel movements were never in short supply.

The shape ahead of him continued at a crawl, always just a step ahead of Timmy.

"Mitchell, wait up!" Timmy yelled in frustration. "What the hell, man?"

The figure at the opposite end of the bathroom stalls had just turned toward the front of the building. Slowly, it turned back toward Timmy, his phone's flashlight illuminating a shaky swath of ground. It was Mitchell, but at the same time it *wasn't*. Part of his forehead was missing, the white skull beneath a terrifying signifier that something was so, so wrong. His tunic hung loosely from his shoulders, and a crimson line of viscous liquid trailed from his mouth down to his costume sword belt.

Mitchell bumbled forward, taking slow steps. A wheeze escaped his mouth, sounding like the hiss of a rattlesnake when you stumble upon their den.

Timmy took it for the warning it was. He backed up, awkwardly retreating into the dark. As he struggled to keep his footing he asked, "Mitchell, what happened to you, man? You—you need a hospital."

Timmy tripped on a jagged root, landing on his back. His walkie burst to life at the same time he yelped in pain. Donnie's voice was tinny, the walkie held too far from his mouth. "Timmy, you there? TIMMY! I had to open the gates by my goddamned self. It's already 9:20, it's a freaking madhouse. Get your ass back here now."

Mitchell's head tilted to the side, as if he was trying to figure out where the noise had come from. He seemed confused, and while he searched, he stopped walking. His mouth clicked open and closed. His jaws snapped and the wheeze still eked past his teeth, as if he was tasting the air.

Timmy let go of the walkie talkie, the cheap plastic landing against a rock with a *crack*. He crab-walked backward in a mad dash to put distance between himself and the ailing Mitchell, the odor coming off the manager so rancid that Timmy's eyes and nose burned.

The frantic motion caught the attention of the stunned Mitchell, who raised his hands before him, reaching out for the prone Timmy. He bent at the waist, a look of hunger attaching itself to his decaying features, mouth still clacking.

Timmy continued in his struggle to get away from Mitchell. He caught his hand against a jagged rock, screaming in pain as one of his nails tore from his fingertip. He dropped down onto his back, panicking as Mitchell drew closer. He balled his hand into a fist, drawing it to his chest. He could already feel the blood pooling in his palm from the stripped nailbed. He wouldn't be fighting, not with that hand.

As Mitchell stopped right above him, Timmy kicked with all his might, feeling something give in the leg he connected with. Mitchell collapsed, practically landing on top of him. He reached his limbs straight out, grabbing for Timmy as his teeth continued to snap.

Timmy rolled away at the last second, using his uninjured hand to push off the ground. Standing, he ran back toward the front of the building.

Was he trying to fucking bite *me?*

Rounding the front of the building, Timmy turned to check that the coast was clear behind him. It was. Mitchell must have been struggling to get back up. Timmy couldn't bring himself to feel bad—something was already wrong with that guy.

The bell above the giftshop doors rang as Timmy pulled on a handle. It wasn't exactly loud, but the guests still hadn't made their way to the area. With Mitchell so close, he feared it would be enough to alert him. Sucking his teeth, the door swung shut behind him, the bell chiming again. He paused; without the set of keys he'd left on Donnie's truck bed, he'd only be able to lock a single door. Timmy figured it was better than nothing. He clipped the locking mechanisms into place and crept away from the entrance.

Toward the back counter, he took in the bottles of fake blood, fake fangs and masks, fake knives, axes, guns, and sickles. The prefabbed Halloween candy bowls with battery-powered hands, glowing red eyes, or cackling witches. The plushies of Hollywood-famous serial killers and final girls, the racks of movie posters, and the blood-glazed coffee mugs. The macabre world around him hit differently as he took them in then. Loving horror—watching it, believing in it—was all fine and dandy, until you started living it.

If Mitchell's grime-speckled skull showing wasn't enough of a sign that something was going on, him trying to eat Timmy's face certainly did the trick. In the movies when it happened, no one ever knew what they were. But this wasn't a movie. Slow moving, cataract eyes, that hissing wheeze and gnawing teeth? Yeah, that was a *zombie*, the undead, a squeaker, a rotter, a riser, the freaking living dead. God *did* proclaim He'd raise the dead in the Bible, right? Timmy had figured that would mean some beloved nun or priest or pope or something. Not *this.* And definitely not here. Not in Cemetery. Not while he made minimum wage at *Scream Fest*.

A crash from the front brought him back to the present horrors. Startling as he turned, Mitchell had found him. Luckily though, he had crashed directly into the locked door, his bucking jingling the bell each time he moved.

Zombies can't open doors, check.

Timmy took a deep breath, almost biting his lip enough to draw a line of blood. He needed to center himself, and then he needed to hide. The second door was still unlocked, and it was a *push* not a pull-to-enter. Michell's weight alone would be enough. Why the hell hadn't he thought to block it? He cursed himself for his stupidity, literally surrounded by usable objects. He was not going to allow himself to be eaten. Especially not by Mitchell of all people. He was the laziest boss Timmy had ever worked under—not that a hardworking boss would necessarily sway his desire to be eaten, but it might.

Timmy ran for the cashier counter, sliding the last three feet to slow himself. He rolled over the counter, dropping off the backside out of sight. His nailbed still bled into his shirt, but his concentration was mostly elsewhere. He realized he was holding his breath, as if that would help. Forcing in hungry gasps of air, he worked quickly to catch his breath in the hopes that breathing normally would be quiet enough.

As Timmy's heart was returning to its typical speed, he whispered a silent prayer for what was to come next. Maybe Mitchell would be distracted by someone else—not that he desired harm to befall others. Timmy just pictured himself speeding away from the fest with all his limbs unbitten. Was this the start of an apocalypse? Because he needed to get home to take care of his elderly mother then. He would not let it end here with *Mitchell*. Poor Fran needed him.

The bell above the front door chimed, the door's inward motion grating on his nerves like nails on a chalkboard. He cursed his stupidity again, this time for his choice in hiding places. There was no back exit.

"Oh my god, that zombie costume is so good!"

"Seriously, that performer deserves a raise." A young woman's voice carried across the quiet giftshop. Could Mitchell have already left? "Wait, why are all the lights off?"

Timmy slowly raised his head above the counter, taking in the two people before him. One was the young woman who had just finished speaking, and the second looked younger, possibly a cousin or sibling. They were wearing horror tee shirts and their makeup was done in dramatic, horror movie fashion. These were fairgoers, so how the hell did they get past Mitchell?

Timmy stood up slowly, as if each inch he moved upward doubled the weight on his shoulders, the pressure building to subdue him. Was he now in charge of these peoples' wellbeing?

The two took in Timmy, their eyes roving from his pale face down to the blood all over his shirt from his torn nail. Then they both smiled brightly at him. "Hi, is there a power outage or something? Nothing's on."

"That man...the—the zombie that you were talking about, where the fuck did he go?"

The older of the two looked taken aback. "Hey, can you cool it with the f-bombs?"

"Sorr—no, we don't have time for this. Answer the question." Timmy was met with blank stares, their growing discomfort obvious. He really didn't have time for this. "Now!"

"Jeez, man, he was standing right at the door trying to get inside. Just like a real zombie would. And those white contacts...so creepy—"

"He's still there now?" Timmy stretched to the top of his height, trying to see around the women. He was growing increasingly agitated; this was unlike anything he had ever experienced. How do you function when you know death is at your literal door? "He just let you pass? Is he still there now?"

"He reached for us and did a *really* good zombie noise, but you guys aren't really allowed to touch us though, right?"

"That's not—he's not—"

The bell chimed again, Timmy's sharp intake of breath caught rough in his throat like splinters of glass. Finally he could see him—the knight of the living dead—maroon tunic and costume sword hanging loose off the desiccated body of Mitchell the manager.

"Listen to me right now." Timmy's whisper might as well have been a shout for how it carried. "You need to get away from him as fast as you can. That's not an actor, it's a real zombie."

Smiling, it dawned on the young woman that Timmy's behavior must have been to sell the realness of the scene. She was still against the cursing, but if it added to her sister's enjoyment, her fear, she'd let it slide.

"Don't just stand there and fucking smile at me. Come on, move!"

The young woman turned to her little sister to insist they play along but was already too late. As she took in her sister's face—for the last time alive—Mitchell's rank, gangrenous hands closed around the little girl's arms. His face came forward in a snap, like a snake latching on to unwitting prey. His teeth parted skin and muscle from the girl's neck, arterial spray covering her older sister's face as she tried to pull away.

The young woman screamed, a heart-rending sound that affected even Timmy in his heightened state. The little girl dropped to the linoleum tile, twitching, spasmodic jerks wracking her body as her lifeblood coated the floor in an ever-widening pool of black. Timmy tried to motion for the woman to come toward him, but he was stuck stock-still in awe of what he'd just seen. The older sister's screaming continued until she seemed on the verge of passing out.

Finally, her voice died out with a bloodied crackle. It was replaced by fiery anger as she grabbed anything she could reach from the surrounding shelves to hurl at the approaching Mitchell. Mug after mug shattered against his face. Yet undaunted, he moved as if it were nothing.

"Just run!" Timmy screamed. For a second, Mitchell's iris-less eyes twitched in his direction. Timmy threw himself below the counter, praying that he had been fast enough. He wanted to help, but he was too much of a coward and he knew it. Another summer had passed by and he still hadn't asked for that raise he'd been dying for. He was no hero. He wasn't even doing a good job of saving his own skin. If Mitchell did get him, he might, Timmy thought with a spot of gallows humor, literally die for that raise.

Another crash came and the young woman yelled, so Timmy knew Mitchell was after her again. He raised just his head above the counter.

The distance between the two had shrunk considerably. The young woman swung a pumpkin-shaped candy basket at Mitchell with all her might, the pressure of each hit doing little to stop him from advancing. She dropped the basket and picked up a Halloween yard sign. It was little more than cardboard and particle; however, the end was carved to a point. In her adrenaline-fueled rage she stabbed it forward wildly. It caught Mitchell in the right cheek, the pointed stake pressing its way through his chomping teeth. She continued to shove it deeper into his gaping mouth, the hissing and moaning coming out as a garble as she reached his throat.

With one final thrust of the stake, she tilted Mitchell off his feet. His body dropped to the bloody floor in a rush. The sign pushed out through the front of his face as the back of his head became flush with the floor. Falling sideways, it plunked into one of the shelves, the end still sticking out of the motionless Mitchell's mouth. A pool of Mitchell's blood spilled out to mix with that of the little girls, his blacker and decidedly thicker and congealed.

Timmy stood up, coming around the corner and grabbing the young woman up in a giant hug. "Holy shit, you freaking killed him."

The woman stood tight in his grip, slipping into shock. Her hair was a frizzy, dirty blonde, though stippled in blood, and her cat eye makeup was accentuated in gore. She was pale, cold, and shivering, and her eyes stared off into nothingness. Timmy remembered reading somewhere that asking someone their name could ground them and pull them back to themselves, back from the ledge they were teetering over. He asked twice before practically screaming it a third time, "hey, what's your name?"

She shook her head as if waking from a dream. Tears broke from the corners of her eyes. "Umm, Mary. It's Mary. That—that was my little sister, Ann."

"Well Mary, you did it, you stopped him. But we still need to get away from here. My name is Timmy, I work here."

Mary blinked rapidly, raising her head and trying to get something out of her eye. Timmy realized it was her own sister's lifeblood. He stepped an aisle over, looking for something she could use as a towel. Almost everything was speckled and splattered in carnage, but one clean Halloween flag caught his eye. He grabbed it.

He couldn't believe what just happened. That this young woman had lost someone so fast, and that it had taken place right in front of him.

Turning back into the aisle he stared in disbelief. Mary stood gazing down at Mitchell, whose mouth had just removed a sizable chunk of her Achilles tendon. She didn't make a sound, just stared with vacant eyes. As her body crumpled toward the floor, the weight becoming too much for her injured leg to support, she looked to her sister's body and smiled.

Timmy knew the amount of blood she was losing was far too much, there was nothing he could do. He slipped in the trio's blood as he stumbled his way down another aisle, eager for the fall air, for the freedom of outside. Again the coward.

He couldn't bring himself to look back. He ran.

Timmy hadn't made it far when the bell rang in the distance. It might have been his mind playing tricks on him, his subconscious picturing the chime of an elevator waiting to drop him straight down to his eternal suffering, but he really didn't think so. He couldn't pinpoint why, but it felt as if Mitchell was after *him* specifically, always just a step behind, beelining for him regardless of what he did. If Timmy hadn't run off before the gates opened to guests, if he wasn't out of the way at the giftshop, would that still feel like the truth? He made it a good quarter mile—Mitchell still nowhere to be seen but undoubtedly there—before settling on a destination. His idea was full of lights, people, and hopefully help.

What most of the *Scream Fest* visitors failed to realize annually was that the grounds were worked into a maze-like winding funnel of buildings, tents, rides, scares, and actual mazes, the design of which accepted you in with open arms, smiled at you liked old friends, and then chewed you up, grinding you through scare after vicious scare before spitting you out at the end. Each bit was delicately built to move you forward with each scream.

The end, the *crème de la crème* of attractions, was the Haunted Ferris Wheel, the height of which allowed parkgoers to see the entire fair, to see fellow thrill seekers running and screaming through the scares they had just experienced. It was considered a *calming* sendoff. The Ferris wheel was gigantic, but even so, the lines were often a long wait. By design, this forced visitors to take in the smells of deep-fried foods, lemonades, beer, and cotton candy from the surrounding food trucks.

That was where Timmy was headed, each step thumping the trodden path below his feet.

As overhead lights illuminated his route, Timmy knew he'd finally made it. He took in the groups of people as he jogged forward. They were everywhere, the sheer number of them bringing tears to his eyes.

He ripped through the crowd, followed by shouts and concerned faces. He raced headlong toward the first drink stand. Stopping before a group of smiling teens, he snatched a large lemonade out of one of their hands, cracking the top and spilling it down the length of his front as he gulped the sweet, cold liquid.

Gulping air as he finished, Timmy wiped his face with a dirty hand. The teens gave him a disgusted look, but in his current state must have thought better of saying something. Their mumbled curses were lost amidst the cacophonous lines.

Timmy took in the crowds around him, not sightseeing but searching. Looking for Mitchell. It was harder than he imagined it would be, the number of costumes and fake blood in the crowd drawing his eye to the wrong people. And getting caught up on something that wasn't Mitchell was a mistake he couldn't afford.

Startling Donnie earlier was a mistake he would pay for. His boss wouldn't trust anything he said, presuming he was just trying to scare him. And although Timmy considered alerting the staff working the stalls, he was afraid it would take them too long to be convinced, assuming it was a prank to tide over the crowd for the long wait times. When everywhere you looked was one horror or another, how were you supposed to convince people of *real* danger?

A scream drew Timmy's attention in the opposite direction. Again, he was too late. Mitchell had arrived—blood soaked and awkwardly dragging his injured leg—but there he was all the same. The teen Timmy had stolen the lemonade from cried out in pain in his grasp, chisel-shaped incisors and canines sinking inches into her shoulder. Blood spurted from the newly parted skin, the sight of which made more than one of the teenagers collapse. Mitchell released her with a hiss, her body dropping heavily to the ground. The tilt of his head made it look like he was searching for something, perhaps even *smelling*.

Of course Timmy had gotten into it with his ex-boss—not for the first time ever, but this boss had turned into some kind of freaking zombie-bloodhound. Had Timmy brought about that girl's demise by stealing her lemonade? How was that possible?

Not waiting to find out, Timmy sprinted off. Every muscle in his legs burned. He hadn't run much since track and field in Cemetery High School, and that was a lifetime ago. He felt soreness in muscles he didn't even know he had, the pull of each step sending aching pains shooting up his body. Better tired than dead.

The startling action did not go unnoticed by Mitchell. The crowd had parted for Timmy like the Red Sea, the waves of people virtually lining a straight shot toward him. Mitchell's brain sent directions to his body to move again, his ankle barely lifting from the ground, scraping grass with each step. He didn't know what urged him on. He knew nothing at all but the drive. The pulsing *need* to feed. And, for some reason, his remaining synapses fired him after Timmy. He moaned at his slow movements, but slow and steady often won the race.

Each time Timmy looked behind him he saw Mitchell. He tried running around groups of people or knocking trashcans into Mitchell's way. It didn't matter the speed at which he ran—which was decreasing rapidly as his lungs pleaded for respite—nor did it help when he zigged, or zagged. He was coming, and there was nothing Timmy could do but flee.

A line of people caught Timmy's eye. In his cowardice, he'd hoped the crowd would allow him to disappear, but nothing was stopping Mitchell. He needed to think, and quickly. The long line meandered toward the Ferris wheel, the rotating booths filled with laughter and camera flashes.

A spark of an idea came, but he knew the timing would have to be perfect.

Jogging around the line, Timmy saw the Ferris wheel operator, Ryan—a guy he was luckily friendly with. As the latest group of riders departed, Timmy called out to Ryan that it was an emergency. Cutting the line, he clamped the little door shut with a snap and prayed Ryan would start the ride without arguing.

The Ferris wheel had conjoined vinyl booths that resembled a fifties diner. The boxcar design gave a 360-degree view, rather than the straight one the ski-lift style models gave. The larger design brought them closer to the ground each revolution, closer to the maddeningly determined Mitchell, but Timmy just needed the reprieve to figure out his next steps.

The Ferris wheel stayed still for what felt like an eternity; the idling motor had Timmy practically panting in anticipation. Mitchell limped his way through the crowd, dragging his foot behind him and moaning as his head tilted from side to side.

A man in line, already angry over Timmy cutting, held a hand out to stop Mitchell, the pressure on the zombie's chest slowing him. He turned toward the man, as if seeing him for the first time. Timmy didn't hear what was being said but could tell from the man's stance that it wasn't nice. For a moment, Mitchell stood completely still. It was as if he was letting the man get out everything he wanted to say before taking his turn. He then sprang into action, gripping the man's wrist before biting through several fingers. Blood sprayed from the nubs; the man's scream audible to all. Mitchell chewed with a crunch of bones before continuing past.

Timmy leaned out the seat, shouting and motioning for Ryan to start the ride. It took precious seconds before Ryan's face finally turned toward him. His eyes were glossed over, stunned at what he had just witnessed. He started the ride in a daze.

The Ferris wheel scraped along its track with a clunk, the kind of sound that should probably turn people off from riding but didn't. It sounded like a chorus of angels to Timmy. Mitchell's decrepit hand had just reached the metal bars before the booth swept out of his reach.

Timmy laughed at the spot of luck. Soon Mitchell would be far below, and he'd have several safe minutes to breathe and think of an escape. He wished he'd run back for the walkie-talkie. He'd dropped it pretty hard but figured he could have gotten it to work. Of course, with hindsight being 20–20, he would have made a lot less mistakes. Wouldn't have followed Mitchell in the first place. At this point, Donnie probably assumed he'd abandoned the job like Jeremy had.

As the Ferris wheel made its first full rotation, Timmy tried to look for Mitchell but didn't see him anywhere. Maybe he'd left? Became centered on someone else? Fallen to his death when the ride took off?

No way was Timmy that lucky.

The lines of waiting people, somewhat structured before, albeit loud, had turned to riotous fleeing. Seeing someone—or some*thing* that used to be a person—chomping down on a fairgoer's fingers had broken the spell that this was all for show.

But on the second rotation, Mitchell stood ready like a harbinger of death. He stood just outside where the booth skimmed the ground, as if he'd been watching, *learning*. He was blood soaked, having killed others waiting in line, and his maroon tunic was slick with the stuff. He was easily distinguishable from those wearing the corn-syrupy alternative, and everyone was doing their best to avoid him. Bumping, shoving, and even trampling had begun in earnest as scared civilians tried to stomp their way to safety.

As Timmy's booth lowered toward the ground, Mitchell latched onto the metal bars with a vicelike grip. The booth continued across the ground, Mitchell's lower half dragging below it. All the while he gnashed his teeth and reached for Timmy, who was cowering as far back as he could get.

The booth took to the air, Mitchell dragged upward with it. His right hand held on as if it had been welded to the bar, his left inching ever closer to Timmy as he raised his body, hefting himself into the seat.

Timmy was out of time and out of options. He kicked Mitchell in a desperate attempt to distance himself, knocking him back out of the seat. Still clinging on with his right hand, Mitchell immediately started to climb again, the moaning and hissing escaping his mouth like evil taunting.

Tears rained down Timmy's face in defeat as Mitchell slithered his way over the bars, his body landing inside the booth with a thump. Timmy looked around for anything that could save him, anything he could use to survive. They were at the top of the Ferris wheel, way too far from the ground to jump.

Would falling to his death be better than being eaten?

Mitchell's body clanged as he raised himself to his feet. No, not his body clanging—the costume sword! Timmy reached for it wildly, bending at an impossible angle to grab the sword while avoiding Mitchell's tireless jaws. His fingers clasped around the pommel of the sword, drawing it several inches from its sheath before it stopped. He had the angle all wrong and was forced to stop as Mitchell snapped too close to his hand.

Feeling around his pockets for anything of use, Timmy settled on his wallet. It was all he had; the small photo of his mother inside his only reminder of what he could make it back to. He waited for Mitchell to lunge with his mouth extended. Timmy smashed the leather wallet into his mouth, Mitchell's teeth sinking in deep before realizing it wasn't flesh. Timmy pressed his forearm up under Mitchell's chin while he was distracted, turning his body, and yanked the sword free.

The wallet fell to the diamond-plate flooring with a plop. Mitchell lumbered forward again, the space between them practically nonexistent. This time Timmy was ready. He raised the costume sword, the point of which slipped directly into Mitchell's open mouth.

Mitchell—simply responding to brainwaves—did all the work. With each step, he slid the sword further into his mouth, finally stabbing into the back of his own throat. The wound made by the yardstick was much smaller than the sword was wide, eventually catching as the sword widened toward the hilt.

Timmy had him; all he had to do was move the handle of the sword around to control the thrashing Mitchell. His teeth still gnashed, but he was powerless as long as the sword was there. Timmy dragged him toward the door of the booth, popping it open, and with a final heave shoved Mitchell out.

Mitchell's brain misfired as he plummeted, empty. As he struck the ground facedown, the sword was forced deeper into his throat, severing his spinal cord and separating the entire top of his head. The light controlling his movements was snuffed out. Dead.

TWO CEMETERY PD OFFICERS stood over the body of the *Scream Fest* manager, which was severely bloody, emaciated, and headless. They had pulled back the sheet to look at him, each one thinking completely different things.

At the same time, one officer said "zombie" while the other said "drugs."

"Oh, come on man. Why didn't the injured people turn then? You remember that Florida highway shit, right? *Bath salts*, man. I'm telling you."

"Haven't reanimated...*yet*."

MR. CODY

My aunt has never been the kind of person to go away on vacation. I wish she hadn't this time.

She's a homebody, through and through. The type that would rather get a fancy dinner delivered at home, lukewarm, than experience the ambiance of the restaurant itself. Or at least that's always how I saw her, thanks to my parents.

So, it comes as quite the surprise when, only weeks after moving into a new house, my mother is asked to housesit while she goes away for two weeks. I don't know why, but to me it feels as if she's running.

The house is on this windy road off the center of Cemetery. I realize that describes a good percentage of the roads in this town, but I'm not really one for descriptions. The house itself is a nice ranch-style with a basement cut into the foundation. It's solid, just dangerously outdated. It is clean though, as my aunt continually brags about it being professionally done. Something about the previous owner passing away in the living room or something like that? It gives me the heebie-jeebies just looking at the place after hearing that.

Apparently, the owner had been elderly, and the realtor assured my aunt there was no foul play. As if that makes it better? I still think about an old guy's death juices seeping into the couch. Not that she kept it or anything, but *eww*.

Luckily, she trashed or sold most of the large items before moving in. The first load was long gone, but she hadn't been able to secure another dumpster on such short notice, so she's been kicking what's left to the curb little by little each garbage day. The side of the house and most of the garage are still lined with thick, black garbage bags of the man's life. I wonder how much of him, how many years, are tucked away in there like so much refuse. Is that really all life has to give? Perhaps. But, on the other hand, he was a very old man with no remaining family. At least he had the chance to live out his remaining years. So, then again, perhaps not.

My mother outright refused to stay at my aunts for the two full weeks, stating that because we only live five minutes apart, she would simply stop in every day.

We spent the first week eating dinner at my aunt's dining room table, a solid wood rectangle that's probably as old as the house itself, and running the laundry in the basement every other night. My aunt jokingly told us that if we heard anything coming from the basement it was okay to ignore it, as it was "just Mr. Cody." And, honestly, the basement did make a hell of a lot of weird noises in that first week. I just assumed it was the old dryer. The kind of old that sounds like you loaded it up with bricks every time it spins round, even though it's drying soft towels.

The washing machine also makes a strange knocking noise every time the spin cycle is on. It's odd, but not the kind of thing that would warrant an exorcism.

And although I'm pretty positive it was a *joke*, something just meant to spook us, I'm unconvinced.

With my aunt away and my mother handling the laundry, I've been elected to ensure the garbage makes it to the curb. My arms and broad chest are slick with sweat, my shirt sticking to my back. I stop, breathing heavy, and run a hand through my wet, curly hair. I've no idea what are in these, but they're heavier than expected. With me dragging loads full of past-life out to the front lawn, my mother's been inside alone for longer than usual.

It's then, as I stand catching my breath, that I hear her screaming inside. My heart stops, my brain going to the absolute worst: a tumble down the stairs, a bad knife cut while washing the dishes, a stroke or heart attack even. Before I can get to the front steps, my mother emerges from the front door, pale with keys in hand.

"What is it? What happened?"

"We'll just finish up with the laundry tomorrow, Charlie. Spooked myself is all."

She locks the door and strides to the car in an act of normalcy. However, I notice she doesn't once look back at the house.

THE FIRST HALF OF our second week housesitting goes like clockwork. No hiccups, messes, or additional screams. The dryer's still groaning in protestation every time it's expected to do its job, and the washing machine's still knocking as if a neighbor's at the door, but that's about it.

A quick Google search shows me that the elderly man who died here was indeed a Mr. Cody, a fact that might have made my aunt's statement creepier, but I just take it as confirmation that it must be a joke. I withhold the information from my mother though.

She eases back into feeling comfortable and, therefore, I allow myself to do the same, figuring not telling her is the best decision I could make.

I have most of the trash out of the garage, which ought to make my aunt happy when she gets home. It'll just be a rather large final garbage day this week, but it should be fine. As I grab the final bags, the door on the house side of the garage pops open. I straighten up, the temperature suddenly dropping. The hairs on the back of my neck and arms stand on end. I cross the garage, sticking my head through the door and call out for my mother.

Her response is muffled, practically inaudible. She's upstairs.

This has happened throughout the past week and a half—the basement door popping open or swinging closed of its own accord. I figure it's something to do with the insane humidity from having the dryer in an enclosed space. Something about air pressure, moisture, and wooden doors, right? But there's also something creepy about it eating away at the back of my mind. It isn't the kind of slow movement you would expect of a door unlatching. It's more decided, a *swing*, as if someone—or some*thing*—is purposefully opening it.

Weird then, that there is never anyone there.

I push it to the back of my mind, latching the door again. Grabbing up the final two bags, I retreat out of the garage, pulling the old overhead door down behind me.

Our final night before my aunt returns is here. My mother and I decide to make it a little celebration. We grab fast food on the way over, figuring the treat will be nice. The only thing we need as we set up the table is two glasses for water. My mother's adamant about this. You can drink anything you want with dinner, but you always receive a water glass. I don't argue as I dig into my chicken sandwich. She alternates between her fries and a burger. The conversation is merry, as if we're about to embark on our own kind of vacation. And honestly, we are.

My aunt hadn't asked me to handle the trash, but I bet she knew I wouldn't just sit idly. We've been doing more wash than usual too, just to have something to keep us here. I'm sure allowing the hamper to fill up a bit is something my mother will be pleased about.

"Now that we're at the end of our time here," I pause, finishing a big bite and swallowing, "I figured it'd be fine to tell you I googled the house."

My mother shifts slightly in her chair, a move denoting her discomfort, but it doesn't register as such for me.

"Why'd you feel the need to do that, Charlie?"

"I don't know. I guess just curiosity?" I reply. I feel her eyes bore into me as I bite my sandwich, fear gripping me as if I ruined the night. I ramble, "like, did you know that that famous detective lives next door? The woman from that giant case in October? You can find anything online these days. I guess that means Aunt Shery will be safe at night...probably didn't even need us housesitting. Oh, and like how the man that died here was actually a Mr. Cody? Aunt Shery didn't make that up."

My mother swallows like she hasn't chewed her food at all, her throat visibly working the food down like a boa constrictor. I think I slipped in that tidbit well, right on the backend of a big reveal, but maybe I didn't?

I feel as if the room has gotten a slight chill to it, and I don't think it's due to my mother.

"You really shouldn't bother yourself with that kind of thing now, Charlie," Mom says. A slight color has crept into her cheeks, and when she sets her burger aside, I have the distinct feeling I've done something terribly wrong.

"I'm sorry, Mom. I was just interested is all. I thought it proved that Aunt Shery was telling a stupid joke. And it's like a little piece of town history too. You don't really believe in ghosts, right? It's not like Mr. Cody's spirit is trapped in the basement of all places."

"No, I do not." My mother's voice is clipped.

I meant well, but it's clear I've touched a nerve. I wonder how I can make her forget what I said, as tonight is supposed to be our little celebration. Our little goodbye to the duty of watching over my aunt's house.

Before I settle on an approach to forgiveness, my mother jumps from her seat. She puts her unfinished food in the trash bin. Scooping up the water glasses from the table, she says, "It's fine, Charlie, forget it," but her voice is breathy, as if she's upset.

I rush to finish my food, the topic of a death in the house not nearly enough to curb my appetite.

My mother starts washing the two glasses under hot water, the soapy sponge squeaking as she aggressively spins it in circles around the ring of the glass. It's weird how you can tell a mother's mood by how hard she washes the dishes, but now I know for sure she's upset with me.

She presses the first sopping, steaming glass into my palm. I take that as her not-so passive-aggressive way of telling me to dry the dishes. I don't argue. What's there to say, anyway? I'm the reason she's angry, even if I don't quite understand why. I grab a couple paper towels and start spinning the glass around to soak up the remaining water. Sitting the first glass on the counter, I proactively take the other from my mother before she can assault my palm with hot glass a second time.

After drying it, I open the cabinet above, placing both snugly inside. I shut the cabinet door with a snap, taking a breath before facing my irate mother. I lean against the empty counter, taking the extra time to collect my thoughts. I turn to face her.

"Look, Charlie, just help me with the dryer so we can get out of here, okay?" She sighs still, but I'm absolutely okay with taking the olive branch.

I lead the way downstairs, the resounding beep of the dryer going off before I hit the bottom step. *Perfect timing*. The humidity from the dryer is already causing a layer of sweat to dampen my forehead. Let's finish this so we can get out of here, indeed.

The load of wash in the dryer's a set of bedding: the worst kind of laundry. And every mother on Planet Earth probably has their own system for how it's supposed to be done. The tedium, the preparation, the care involved, and yet it's never correct, never enough for Mom. That's the demanding nature of folding a bedsheet.

That I understood. That I'm prepared for. I had accepted my fate in the trenches of laundry folding long before today.

What I'm not prepared for is the following events.

The basement door slams shut with a *bang*. The hinges shake with the force of it. My mother screams in shock. The door shutting has cut out most of the light, leaving us with just the overhead bulb in the corner of the room.

My breath catches in my chest. You never expect a door to slam shut when the only other occupant in the place is standing next to you.

However, I manage to keep the scream tamped down, my mother beating me to the punch anyway. I grab her arm to steady her, to steady myself.

The look in her eyes is anything but calm.

"It's probably just the humidity in here, the basement door to the garage has been doing the same," I say, more for myself than her. "I'll check it out."

I head for the door down here first, figuring if it's not stuck, at least the light inside will help us to finish up. But the door is stuck, jammed up tight. I can't see the garage light through the cracks around the door, and somehow, it's as if it's melded into the wall.

I head back to my mother, her eyes still wild with fright. She stands in the center of the basement, arms wrapped around herself as if for protection. She shakes her head frantically when her eyes land on me coming around the corner.

"Charlie, we need to get out of here." She's panicking, rational thoughts abandoning her. "Now, Charlie, now!"

I shake her gently by the shoulders. "Mom, take some deep breaths. It's because of all the humidity, I promise."

"No, Charlie," she replies. "No, it's not."

I can tell from what she doesn't say that she's seen this before.

"Mom...what happened the day you ran out of the house?"

She eyes me, as if I've cracked the code. Hit the mark.

The washer door pops open, rusty hinges creaking as it sways. The machine knocks over and over.

Knock. Knock. Knock. Knock!

The door continues to swing open and closed like a cavernous, monstrous mouth. I've always hated these front loader machines, feeling like I'm filling a gluttonous gob or making some kind of sacrifice. The fact they always seem to be in dank, faraway basements makes me think of Indiana Jones by way of *The Twilight Zone*. Except unlike Indy, I'm not seeking adventure, and I've no clue what to do now.

The knocks continue, like overloud burps, and water projectile shoots out toward my mother and me. The splash that whips my knees is painful enough that I wince. My mother backs away as fast as she can, vibrating from head to toe.

"This," she says, her teeth chattering in fear. "*This* is what started to happen."

"It's old and on its last leg, it's probably just got a rusted-out pipe or something spitting water. That's all—"

I trail off as another blast of water, this time more like a flood, shoots out, sweeping me off my feet. I'm propelled by the force of the water until my back hits the basement wall across from the machine. It hurts, but I'm so astonished it barely registers.

The next torrent spits out at an alarming rate. The basement, cut into the foundation, has taken on water, filling like a concrete swimming pool. I realize I can no longer see my mother. I frantically search for her, my breath held in panic.

She surfaces with a crash, eye makeup carving black lines down her face. It adds to how frightened she appears, but I'm pretty sure that, like me, the jet of water knocked her down, nothing more.

I stand up, the water already above my knees. We have to get out of here, and soon.

As I wade toward my mother in the dark, the old dryer turns on. The door is open, and the spinning tumbler starts rapidly heating water. The rise in temperature is immediate. Another couple of minutes and it could reach a boil.

"Mom, we have to get out of the water," I cry. "Now!"

I reach her, and she's a shaking mess. I am too. We move together toward the stairs, fighting the growing waves. The water spitting from the washer pulls while the cycling dryer creates an artificial undertow. Any deeper and it'll be hard to stay afloat.

I help her climb onto the base of the stairs. She shivers, petrified, but she's no longer directly in the flow. I climb up next and see the skin around my ankles has started to pink, smarting from the rising water temperature.

I draw in a breath and try wiping my palms on the thighs of my wet jeans. I think I'm going into shock. My mother definitely is. I step farther up the staircase, taking it in for what feels like the first time. We never really think about things like that, do we? And when we do, it seems to be at the strangest times.

Stairs are just a way to get from floor to floor, we never really inspect them. But as I look at them now, they seem to grow from the basement floor upward into infinity, the darkened door above extending ever farther from me. Maybe that is a sign I should catch onto.

I don't. I thought the door meant salvation.

I tamp down my panic and climb the stairs. Water continues running off me, making my shoes squeak and slip on the painted wood. At the top, the door handle twists freely, but nothing happens when I apply pressure. It doesn't feel as if anything blocks it, nor pushes back. It just doesn't budge. Not even an inch.

I try again, applying more pressure. Still nothing.

I take the largest step back the staircase will allow and drive my shoulder forward with all my might. The wood makes the barest thudding sound but doesn't even move enough to creak.

Did the slamming door damage the hinges or something? I know I saw the entire structure buckle, but damn.

Then, I hear something. A creaking, muffled by the door, but definitely there.

"Hello, is someone there? This isn't funny! I suggest you open the door and leave. Please." My voice sounds weak even to me. This whole situation is under my skin, crawling like fevered ants.

In answer, a glass smashes into the back of the door, the collision of which makes the door move more than my shoulder did. I stare blankly at it as another glass smashes into oblivion on the other side.

One. Two.

Two glasses? Didn't we just wash and put those glasses away?

Yes. I know for a fact that I put them away, even closed the cabinet after. I'm *certain*.

What's going on? Why would somebody mess with us?

"This isn't funny! Open this door right now," I yell, the volume of which hurts my throat. "A pipe is broken down here or something. If you don't let us out, we could get seriously hurt!"

One look behind me is all it takes. My mother has been climbing each step as the water rises. The top of each wave gives off a layer of fog, or is evaporating, I'm not sure which. But I am sure now that the water is too hot to touch. I imagine us as lobsters, dangling over a boiling pot.

I bang my fists on the door, hoping the urgency of my action will sway them if my words can't.

Sweat stings my eyes, the air has grown so hot. Bubbling heat pits and spits around the wooden stairs, getting dangerously close to my mother's shoes. I bang my fists again.

Footsteps approach the door. I can hear what sounds like breathing on the other side. I step back, but I can't see a pair of feet blotting out the kitchen light. There's no one there, and yet...

It's not like Mr. Cody's spirit is trapped in the basement of all places.

But we are.

BESTGHOST

A Novelette

Originally released as a reader magnet in 2023, then rereleased wide as a sample story in 2024.

THE DRIVE

The town of Cemetery ripped past them as they took another turn at speed. The woods, with their changing leaves, melted into colorful blurs. The cool autumn air streamed into the car from the cracked window, Devon flicking the ash off the end of his cigarette. Neither of them had ever been out this far, but the GPS was taking the wheel. The setting afternoon sun, low in the sky, created a blinding reflection.

"I really wish you wouldn't smoke in here. My dad'll beat my ass," Sean said.

"I told you already man, the smell will be long gone by the next time that dude comes to Cemetery," Devon said with a laugh.

"But if my aunt smells the car, she'll definitely tell him."

"Well it's a long drive dude. You want me to just sit and suffer?" Devon asked, a fake quiver to his lip that Sean, driving, completely missed. "Anyway, it's your dad's car, she has no reason to go into it. He bought you the car. Hell, he buys you anything you want just so he can leave again."

Sean opened his mouth to answer then thought better of it.

They drove in silence for several miles, neither wanting to disturb the quiet peace between them. The breeze from the cracked window blew Sean's blonde hair across his pale forehead. He was shorter than Devon, but not *short*, it was just hard to compete with height like that. His slightly muscular arms from years of forced sports, courtesy of his father, were the only things he felt he held over Devon.

Devon was tall, over six feet, and every day brought him closer to being rained on first for the rest of his life. His hair was cropped much closer to his scalp than Sean's, his dark skin another difference between the two. They had been best friends since the day they were born, or at least as far back as either of them could remember.

As they rounded what the GPS marked the final turn, they watched in anticipation of their destination.

"So why this place again?" Devon asked, still pouting.

"The Old Mayor's Mansion is a hot spot for all the shitty kids, druggies, and apparently sometimes homeless people of Cemetery, but—"

"So why are we going there?" Devon asked, cutting off Sean.

"Well, if you would shut up and let me finish!" Sean replied. "The Old Mayor's Mansion is considered a hot spot for paranormal activity. It's one of those spots that people claim just draws spirits to it, like a siphon for ghostliness."

"Still don't see why we have to go to some busted up place," Devon whined.

"It's for the channel, dude," Sean replied. "*The* most haunted place in Cemetery? Why wouldn't the best ghost hunters in the Hudson Valley investigate it? That's why we're called *BestGhost Hunters*. It's not just some stupid name," he shifted in the driver's seat, indignant.

"Oh, it's pretty stupid, Sean."

"Yeah, yeah, yeah. You're the skeptic, Devon, I know. That's fine, it's good for the channel anyway."

"Can't be skeptical of something that simply doesn't exi—" Devon cut off as they turned up the end of the driveway.

The Old Mayor's Mansion grew into existence before them. The Victorian-era mansion had tall peaking roofs and a giant porch that wrapped around to the back. The front of the house seemed to grow out of the porch, the entire bottom floor lined with beams that led to a sweeping roof. The second floor had a balcony, the roof above it much smaller than the first, making way for large windows on either side. The next floor, presumably an attic, featured conical windows and wood, with the roof above ending in a large turret.

It looked beautiful, but as they drove closer they noticed the dilapidation.

The cracked white paint peeled off in strips in some places and had turned a discolored rust in others. The porch's boards were cracked and pitted at odd angles, some missing entirely. Even some of the upper windows were smashed in or missing.

"*Jeeez-us*, Sean, are you sure this place is even safe to enter?"

"I told you, it's a popular spot for dares and investigations. Come on, I promise it's fine," Sean urged.

NIGHT ONE

Sean called out "Action!" as he clicked the remote's record button, smiling into the now-live camera. An array of equipment and cords sat before them on a fold-out table they had brought.

"Hi all. I'm Sean Metlan, and this is—"

"I'm Boomer!" Devon yelled over him.

Sean flushed, his cheeks turning red. "You're really still going for this persona thing? It's not necessary, I promise you."

"It's a bit—a sell, dude. Don't harsh my mellow. All the good hunting shows have a thing—this is just my thing. I'm Boomer. The other ghost hunters out there are going to know me as Boomer, and that's final. You're ruining the video!"

"We'll just edit around it, stupid. Ugh." Sean took a deep breath, holding before the release. He shook himself and tried to loosen up, the color finally leaving his cheeks. "Take two, camera!"

"Hi all, I'm Sean Metlan, and this is Boomer." Devon, having won, smiled brightly into the camera. "We're here to prove that we're the best ghost hunters out there, or as you've come to know us from our channel name, *BestGhost*! We're so thankful for all of your comments, emails, calls, and messages, but unfortunately Sumera is still unwell and will not be joining us again. Her parents think it's for the best, and we will respect that.

Rudy, our trusty canine protector will also be away, as he was Sumera's family dog." Sean broke eye contact with the camera and coughed, saliva catching in his throat.

"Do you think they'll allow Rudy visits to the loony bin—"

"All joking aside," Sean cut in over Devon, "we wish her well and miss her even more than the fans do!" His voice cracked, but he clenched his jaw and kept his eyes dry.

Devon, now Boomer, stepped up to cover. "Many of you may have already watched our intro video for the new equipment Sean's dad got for us, but for those of you that haven't, please check out the link below—and we will also run through it now, so that you know what we're experimenting with today! So Sean, what is this alien-looking soup can?"

Devon smiled, but Sean was annoyed with how he was starting this. "Well, *Boomer*, that is called a REM-Pod. It's an EMF proximity detector, which means it gives off a field of electromagnetic energy, and if something penetrates that field—human, spiritual, or otherwise—the Pod will beep, noting a disturbance. Closer, or continual, interruptions in the field will elicit a heightened beep. It can also detect changes in temperature, which is what this light on top dictates."

"Wow, Sean, that seems pretty *scientific*," Devon sarcastically replied, smiling too wide.

"You all know Boomer, our resident skeptic! It *is* scientific, but we know that won't be enough for you. That's why we have more to show. Want to hand me that next one there?" Devon passed it to him, and Sean held it up for the camera to take in. "This here, folks, is an EMF reader. Nothing you all haven't seen before, but we got a new, fancier one thanks to my dad. This one looks a little more like a walkie talkie, but it has all the bells and whistles the other one didn't. This one can read *and* differentiate between natural and manmade EMF readings, something our other one didn't seem to do. It can also read temperature changes in the air, and the device itself has way more lights and indicators for each reading."

“So...it’s a handheld REM-Pod?” Devon said, laughing.

“This one is a reader, not a field projector. However, the two of them together, giving the same readings, will be much harder to dispute for all the nonbelievers out there like our Boomer here.” Sean laughed too, happy for the recovery. “And the next one, please.”

Devon picked up what looked like a mini old school radio, or a miniature jukebox. Sean took it, holding it out for the camera again, looking pleased with himself.

“This one here is a Spirit Box, but it isn’t the run-of-the-mill kind! We’ve gotten our hands on one of the latest designs. This here, to keep it simple, is a radio. The radio is set up with a device that allows it to scan radio frequencies at an incredible rate. It’s believed that spirits can use the energy it gives off to power through the ether, communicating through words pushed through the radio. It’s super cool, and unbelievably creepy when it happens. And to put any growing arguments to rest from the cynic standing next to me, the radio scans frequencies at such a fast rate that it’s pretty much impossible for a string of words to come out coherently...unless something else is reaching out.”

Devon shook his head and scoffed, but Sean would cut that out later. This was science, so why couldn’t the straightforward mind of his stupid friend see that? *Real* science, a chance to get real proof. Shouldn’t everyone want to do that? Especially a skeptic...

“Oh, and as our lovely Sumera would always remind us, we have plenty of Maglites too, and we are also bugging the place! We will place recording devices all over the house while we investigate, including on our persons, to ensure that anything that may want to reach out and answer our questions can do so. This will ensure that we miss literally nothing as we go back and listen during edits. Thanks for watching, and we cannot wait to start investigating the Old Mayor’s Mansion!”

They broke apart and Sean shut the camera off. He took a deep breath, trying to calm himself after Devon’s shitty jokes. As a skeptic, he expected Devon to not believe, of course, not to mention that added to the channel's believability anyway, but did he really have to be such an ass all the time?

"Wait, can I ask you something?"

Caught off guard, Sean grunted in the affirmative.

"Why the Old Mayor's Mansion?"

"What do you mean why? You've heard the stories your whole life, same as me." Sean was getting irritated.

"Yeah, of course, but what about the channel? These people have never even heard of Cemetery, let alone have a reason to know the stories about this place, right?" Devon said, looking genuinely curious.

Sean sighed, replacing a recorder back onto the supply table. "I guess that's a really good point, dude. We should do another intro clip where we give the story of the place for the watchers. Let's do that now before the light changes."

Devon and Sean did their best to set themselves up in the same places as before. Sean was big on things like that, and even though Devon couldn't be bothered, he did so without complaint. Sean really believed in the whole ghost thing, and although Devon would never understand, he *did* understand money. Sean was also a firm believer in the channel getting monetized, and that was enough of a hook for Devon. Not to mention that, without Sumera, it would be an even split now.

"Ready...and...action," Sean called out, not bothering to check if Devon actually was ready. He clicked the record button and smiled wide at the camera. "So the place we are investigating tonight is called the Old Mayor's Mansion. It's one of the biggest paranormal hot spots in the entire town of Cemetery! We figured we'd give a short history lesson for those that haven't heard of it, and I hope that even if you have, you'll give us just a few minutes to tell you the *real* story of how this all started. Devon, would you like to do the honors?"

Devon smiled at Sean as he said, "Oh, well, as the story is based on *researchable facts*, Sean, I'd love to. Well guys, as you can probably imagine, the story starts with Cemetery's old mayor. Just how old, you ask? The Old Mayor's Mansion was built back in 1878. Yes, folks, that long ago! At the time, he was an incredibly popular figure in the town, so beloved that the people would do anything for him. What most people at the time did not realize was just how dark his home life would become. Mayor Ratchett was a husband and father of six. In all public appearances, they were a model family—idolized even. They were often spoken of as holding hands, being a true unit. Until one bone-chilling night in the middle of January." Here, Devon paused for suspense, looking over to Sean and giving him a nod to continue.

Sean sprang into action, taking the reins. "January sixteenth was a date no one expected to be burned into the history of Cemetery, but horror doesn't often wait to be invited in. The following morning, when Ratchett's driver arrived to bring him to town, there was no answer at the door. As you can imagine, with a family of eight, it was incredibly unlikely that *no one* would answer the door. Knowing the mayor never missed a day of work, the driver immediately worried that something had happened. At the time, there was only a single road leading all the way to the mansion—think of it like an incredibly long driveway. The town's archives claim that the driver tried the door, which was open, and what he found inside haunted him until the day he died.

"The family was murdered during the night. Every. Single. One. The newspapers reported they were on the hunt for a man, but all of the descriptions were weak. It's debated whether someone slipped in during the dead of night. The murderer used the family's own wood cutting ax. They had used the back end of the ax to bludgeon them, rather than the edge, almost as if it were meant to be personal in its brutality. For years, the townspeople thought it was the mayor that had done it, mostly because his injuries were so different from those of the family, but a more recent study claims it's because he was the only family member to wake up. The only one to fight back—to struggle. The driver entered the house to find all eight of the family members murdered—blood, bone, and brains everywhere. The only family member out of bed was the father, who was found bloodied on the couch. The murderer even left the family ax sitting against one of the walls.

"Since that day, the house has been sold no less than a dozen times, each new resident reporting noises, disturbances, and missing items. Most fled before reselling. It's believed that the family, in their anger over what happened to them, never left. That they are still searching for answers. As you can imagine, if those rumors are true, an entire family of eight not moving on would most definitely be a strong enough pull to make a paranormal hot spot such as this."

"However, fast forward many years and the house stands derelict and abandoned—enter us! *BestGhost*, the best damn ghost hunters out there," Devon finished.

He had said it while pulling a face, but Sean still thought it was a good finish. He clicked off the camera again.

"Alright, we need to get these recorders spread around and then we have to get some more lights up. It's getting dark, but we should be good to go. What do you think?"

"I am ready for a night in the dark alone with you, dude," Devon replied with a laugh, grabbing some recorders.

For the next hour, they tried their best to perfectly space out the recorders, focusing on each room, as well as certain spaces that had been rumored to be paranormal portals: the stairwell leading to the second floor, the basement, and the youngest son's bedroom. Each of these specially marked areas received more than one recorder. The lights they set up were focused mostly in the main entryway where they had filmed their introductions, the space acting as their base of operations. Otherwise, each *BestGhost* member had a headlamp strapped on, as well as a handheld camera with night vision capabilities. They would remain in the dark, to offer the best chance of communing with the deceased. The fans seemed to like seeing Sean get scared whenever he heard something. Or at least thought he heard something.

The last sliver of sun stuck with them as they finished and met in the entryway. They were winded from lugging the stuff out of the car and running through the house. A part of each of them thought of Sumera. The techier of the three, she at least had told them what to do with confidence. The two of them were winging it with a prayer. Luckily, with Sean's dad bankrolling, most of the equipment was quality enough that as long as it was facing the right way, it would film what needed to be filmed.

"Think we could have a pizza brought out here?" Devon asked.

"Are you ever not being a smartass?"

"What do you mean?" Devon asked, not a hint of sarcasm or comedy on his face. "I'm hungry and the sun is hanging on like its life depends on it. So I was simply wondering if you thought we could get a pizza delivered here. I'd pay and everything."

"Okay—then no. I doubt that this is within delivery range of any pizza places. Even if you could get them to take you seriously with the address," Sean replied, a hint of shame in his tone for assuming the worst of Devon.

"Well, I'm going to go out to smoke and give it a try anyway, okay?" Devon said, crestfallen.

"Yeah, sure, whatever you wanna do."

Ten minutes later, Devon came back inside with a shit-eating grin. "I found a place. Delivery kid was a fan of *BestGhost*, if you can believe that! Said he'd feed his boss some BS and get the pizza to us. I got pepperoni, hope that's good for you too. He said it might be a while though, so we might as well start."

Sean led them down the hall toward the stairwell. He clicked on his headlamp, making sure it was angled correctly. With Devon being so tall, it was always a struggle not to blind him.

They clicked on their cameras, making sure the night vision was on, and panned across the hall.

"We're here at the Old Mayor's Mansion, and the investigation is about to begin." Sean paused so he'd have a spot to cut while editing. "My name is Sean, and this is my friend Boomer. We're just here, reaching out, to see if anyone would like to communicate with us. Or through us to someone else. Can you repeat our names back to us?"

An all-too-familiar silence reached them. It stretched out through the dark like reaching arms, spreading out and clawing its way down the hall. If you waited long enough, even silence could sound like noise.

"Again, that was *Boomer* and Sean. Repeat our names back to us, or maybe tell us your own name?"

Several minutes passed and nothing happened. Not even a creak in the old wood.

"Well, they aren't very talkative yet, but it's still early. Not even completely dark out."

At that exact moment, Devon's stomach growled loudly, announcing his hunger to the house and the *BestGhost* audience. The two friends laughed heartily at the break in the silence.

"While we wait for the impending arrival of the pizza, we're going to try out a device that may help the spirits of the house reach out." Sean picked up the device, clicking it on and speaking loudly over the deafening shifts in the radio channels. "This is called a Spirit Box. The channeled radio stations are known to create an energy, possibly allowing you, the spirits, to alter the radio frequencies to communicate more easily with us. Are you ready to give it a shot? I'll sit it right here," he finished, placing the small box on the edge of the steps.

For some reason, no one had thought to make the Spirit Box function at a more reasonable volume. Going from dead silence to the cacophonous radio shifts was always a jarring experience. Devon hated the thing, considering it absolute bullshit anyway. Sean had heard of a new one coming out that filtered the channels with less static, but the volume was still at max for some reason, so he hadn't waited to buy.

The channels flickered through, random noises and voices breaking through, but nothing of worth. Nothing they could understand. Sean would give it time, let the energy build for the spirits before they gave up.

More time passed and, just as Devon was about to open his mouth to put an end to the intense level of noise, the radio channels started clicking together, as if they were being strung into a consistent rhythm. No real words were formed, but the consistency struck him as odd. Not odd enough to believe in ghosts—he wasn't an idiot—but definitely odd. No doubt explainable in a scientific, *real* way.

Still, Devon kept quiet.

Minutes passed, with the odd consistency shifts sometimes fading away before coming back, more repetitive each time. Finally, the shifting settled into a loud bleat. It rang out twice in fast succession before the Spirit Box died out.

Sean jumped up and grabbed the Spirit Box, turning it over in his hands and looking for a reason why it would have malfunctioned. He tried turning it back on. Nothing happened.

It was completely dead.

Face pale, Sean said, "I know I'm the believer, and it will inevitably sound like I'm just crying ghost, but didn't that sound an awful lot like 'Sean'?"

"I-I don't know. That was weird. I mean, yeah it could have been 'Sean', but without reviewing, without it happening again, how can we prove that?" Devon asked.

Sean ran a hand through his blonde hair. "I just asked what it sounded like to you, not if it was resounding proof, dude. That's what I heard though. My name, pretty damn clear, two times in a row before the Spirit Box shit out."

In answer, Devon ran his hand down his face, shaking his head. Truth be told, he didn't know what to say. It *had* sounded like "Sean", but that's the thing, it *sounded like* didn't mean it was. He took the Spirit Box from Sean's hands and tried to turn it on and off himself. Nothing.

A feeling of dread momentarily overtook him. Sean's dad wouldn't have bought them something cheap, and cheap to him was expensive for other people. So either he got ripped off, or something weird was going on with the equipment. Just like everyone else in the world, he had heard about faulty equipment around paranormal energies and beings, but he had always chalked it up as BS. But what if—in the smallest, littlest sliver of *maybe* available—it wasn't BS? Devon swallowed hard, passing the Spirit Box back to Sean and trying to put on a face like he couldn't be bothered.

The doorbell clanged through the house as if each bell were on the verge of falling out of the walls. Devon screamed—actually screamed as if someone were there to murder him. He bent over, placing his hands on his knees and taking deep breaths.

Laughing, Sean smacked him on the shoulder. "Got spooked? That's never happened to you before!"

"We. Are. Definitely. Editing. That. Out," Devon said through gritted teeth, trying to save face as his cheeks burned.

Sean reached the front door, Devon right behind him. He thought it was a little weird that the pizza delivery kid would ring the doorbell when he knew it wasn't their house. Maybe it was delivery etiquette or whatever?

Twisting the handle, Sean pulled it open and saw...nothing. No one. He looked left and right, wondering what was going on. He knew squatters and kids often came here, but they had checked they were in the all-clear first. This wasn't exactly a close destination for random ding-dong ditchers, either.

Devon pushed passed him, bending over and picking up a pizza box from the front porch. "Free pizza, cool!"

"This is weird, isn't it?"

"Kid said he liked the channel, didn't he? Probably figured we were investigating and didn't want to bother us more than just a ring of the doorbell. Seems pretty cool to me, seeing as I was going to pay!"

Sean followed Devon back into the entry room. They sat against the wall under the front windows. Devon balanced the pizza box on his knees, propping it up before popping the lid. The pizza was still steaming, the cheese browned and bubbled. Perfect.

"Gotta love a pizza place with a good delivery bag!" Devon practically yelled before shoving his first slice into his mouth. After chewing and swallowing his first bite, he leaned his head back in obvious bliss.

Sean shook off the weird feeling in his stomach and grabbed a slice. No point in wasting perfectly good pizza. And it was a ghost investigation, wasn't it? Of course, he was already a little on edge. This stuff always spooked him. "Not sure if we'll just edit out all of this or not, but maybe we should save some of it for like *BestGhost* B-roll or something?"

"Like, *Pizza with BestGhost*?"

"Something like that," Sean replied.

Half an hour later, the pizza box was empty and their stomachs were overfull. Sean groaned, but Devon sat contentedly with his head against the windowsill. That was the problem with ordering a pizza to a haunted house that wasn't yours...you couldn't exactly save any for later. Not that they had wanted to.

A loud thump sounded from the floor above them, followed by another and another. It sounded like heavy feet smashing into the old and creaky floorboards. Sean and Devon looked at each other, paling. The thumps were followed by a consistent beeping that kept getting louder.

"What the hell is that?"

Sean looked stricken. "I didn't tell you, but when we were setting up the audio recorders, I also left the REM-Pod upstairs. That's it going off now."

"No, I know what *that* sounds like." Another thump sounded above them. "*What the hell is that*? A rat?"

"A rat making that much noise, Devon?"

"A raccoon? A fox?"

"On the second floor of the house?" Sean responded.

"Well, then what the hell is it?"

"Only one way to find out..."

They crept down the hall toward the stairs. They were solid wood, beautiful at one point, perhaps, but rickety and pockmarked now. The wood appeared weak and strained under their feet. The handrail was solid wood as well but had the look of a splintery death trap, the stain all but gone. As they made their way to the top, the thumping and noise from the REM-Pod stopped entirely. Gone. The silence was almost creepier than the unexplained noises.

"Where did you put it?" Devon asked, mostly so that Sean would have to lead.

"Come on," Sean said, pushing past him and heading for the first bedroom of the second floor. He was a firm believer in ghosts—that was why he did what he did—but part of him felt sure this had to be some kind of prank. That much noise, that consistently? It felt phony.

As Sean made it to the bedroom, he froze. He had been so certain that this was a prank that he hadn't thought about the implications. What if it were some crazed squatter who wanted their equipment and money? What would they do? What was the squatter going to do?

Why the hell was the bedroom door swinging closed?

"*Uhhh*" was all Sean could squeeze out.

Devon gripped his arm like it was the last thing he would ever do. "Shit, I'm the one that is supposed to be the skeptic, right? Cause this is spooky as hell."

"Skeptic? Devon, I'm pretty sure there's some crazy squatter messing with us on the other side of the door."

"Oh," Devon replied, straightening up. "That's actually way less scary."

Easing the door back open with his foot, Devon strode into the bedroom like he owned the place. Whether it was an act, Sean couldn't say, but he was fine with giving over the lead.

The bedroom was exactly how Sean had left it. A large canopy bed was off to the right, centered against the wall. The dresser to the left was covered in dust so thick it looked like it was the original color. The accompanying mirror was much cleaner. The two of them stared back at themselves for a moment before Devon stepped away.

"There's no one here and this isn't one of the rooms with broken windows. So what the hell shut the door?"

Devon turned back toward Sean, who was holding a dirty sheet in his hands. "I don't know, but this sheet was covering that mirror when I was up here earlier."

Sean looked green, eyes wide with fear.

"I know it was secure because I checked, knowing that it would scare the hell out of me in the dark."

"It's just a sheet, dude. The wind or something probably just pulled it down," Devon replied, still much calmer, thinking it was a natural threat.

"You—you just said the windows aren't broken in this room, right?"

"Well yeah I did, but maybe it wasn't as secure as you thought."

A thought struck Sean and he turned back to the bedroom. "And where's the REM-Pod? No one would have gotten out past us, right? So what shut the door and where's our equipment?"

Devon got down on his knees and leaned down, using his hands to keep himself from completely going prone. He looked to the left and scanned the wall. Finding nothing, he did the same on the right side. "There! It rolled under the bed is all."

"The REM-Pod was sitting flat on the ground, dude. There was no way for it to roll," Sean said, sounding more and more hysterical.

"Well it's right there, dude, calm down. No need to cry about it, just your ghost friends kicking the equipment around. They don't respect us yet, clearly." Devon stretched forward and picked up the REM-Pod.

At first, he thought there was nothing wrong with it, but upon closer inspection he realized one bulb for the proximity monitor was shattered. Now how did that happen if it had just rolled under the bed? The creepy feeling from earlier inched its way back up Devon's neck. Sean was right after all; no one could have gotten by them. It was impossible. So what had done this?

Sean looked like he was going to vomit. He still had a green tinge to his skin, and he was sweating profusely, his eyes huge and unfocused. Devon needed to take the reins, and fast.

"Well, all our fellow *BestGhost*-ers," Devon began, focusing his camera on the REM-Pod. "As you can see, we have lost the use of one of our most precious investigation tools, as Sean loves to remind us! Therefore, we will have to call it a night and get a repair job. I'm hoping it's a simple bulb switch, but we'll see. Good news for you all, though, is that our investigation of the Old Mayor's Mansion will have to be a two-parter!"

Sean shook his head. Whether he meant he was good to go now or he couldn't handle a second night, Devon wasn't sure, but he was forging ahead either way.

“That’s right! *BestGhost*’s first ever two-part investigation. What a lucky bunch you all are!”

Devon dropped the camera act, looking over at Sean and taking a breath. “You good, dude? Let’s get out of here for now, even if it is just a squatter.” He took the REM-Pod and the audio recorder before patting Sean on the back and guiding him from the room.

“Yeah—yeah, that sounds good,” Sean said. “We’ll do another night.”

“I’ll clean up, you just get the car ready, alright? This could be cool, getting to analyze some of the recordings *before* we’re done for once.”

Sean nodded along, but Devon wasn’t entirely sure he was hearing him.

With the car loaded up, the two headed home. Sean stayed awfully quiet.

The audio they analyzed later made it all the harder to return for a second night.

NIGHT TWO

Regardless of what was in the house last time, a quick scan told them they were alone. Devon secured the front and back door, hoping to alleviate Sean's worry. It was as if he had expected the front door to burst open at their approach, a ghastly moaning coming out in a blast of chilled air.

It wasn't like that though. As they turned up the driveway, the place looked exactly the same as the evening before—the sun being down the only noticeable difference. They let out a collective sigh, perhaps having expected more. Not that they weren't relieved.

They had reviewed all the audio, finding hours and hours of nothing, until they finally reviewed the audio recorder taken from the upstairs bedroom. Right up until the point when they finished the pizza, there was absolutely nothing but silence on the recorder, not even a creak. But then, just as they had heard, there was the thumping of footsteps. On the recorder though, they sounded much clearer, almost as if someone were pacing within the room itself.

Then, right before it cut out, they caught the back end of what sounded like "*...and in my house*". They had stared at each other in dumbfounded silence. They rewound it at least a hundred times before they finally accepted that it really did sound like what they were hearing. It was muffled, staticky, and sounded as if it could be at least a dozen other things, just like every other ghost investigation audio, but the fact that Devon wasn't putting up any kind of convincing argument was more than enough for Sean.

There had been something there, and it was their job to uncover what it was.

They took the time to set up the lights in the entryway and the recorders all around the house and to do a last-minute check on all the equipment before they started.

The REM-Pod hadn't been an easy fix. As weird as Cemetery was, it didn't have a ghost hunting shop of any kind, so they were sadly waiting out the parts order. There was nothing to do about it, so they decided to do the second night without it.

"I think we better start in that bedroom. We can do the Maglite test because we don't have the REM-Pod?"

"Yeah, okay."

Upstairs, the house was quiet. Dead silent. Every step they took sent reverberations throughout the entire mansion. Sean couldn't imagine living here with all this noise. He kept the thought to himself though, figuring Devon would just make some snide remark about his father's money. Yes, he was rich, but Sean elected to live with his aunt—in her much smaller house—because his father was *never* home. He couldn't live with the emptiness. The lack thereof.

Without realizing, Sean walked right into the bedroom, his ruminations completely keeping his mind off the spookiness at hand. He slipped the bag off his shoulder, removing two Maglites and passing one to Devon.

"And for our new *BestGhost*-ers here, Sean, what are these used for again?"

"Right, right. So, Boomer, you take these regular Maglite flashlights, placing them in between the 'on' and 'off' position like this. This in-between position allows for them to turn off and on with the littlest touch or influence. It's believed you can communicate with spirits by getting them to turn one or the other on and off consistently, the energy needed being practically nonexistent."

"So basically the least scientific method of all time?"

"Ah, haven't you all missed him being the skeptic?" Sean played for the camera. "It's much better than him screaming about a pizza delivery, right?"

"I told you we were editing that out!"

"And I do the editing!" Sean laughed as his best friend's face blanched. He continued on before Devon could fire back. "So, folks watching, I think it's time to start tonight's investigation." He gave Devon a stern look, then turned toward the bed and flashlights.

"Hi, my name is Sean, and this is Devon, aka Boomer. We are just trying to communicate with any spirits, anyone that may still be within this house. If there is someone here with us now, can you turn on the right flashlight? All you have to do is give it a little tap. One touch."

The left flashlight popped on.

"Okay...alright. I suppose if you are currently on the bed that could be the right, but I mean the flashlight to *my* right."

The left light flashed off, the right one almost immediately turning on.

Sean gave Devon a serious look.

"A single time is hardly proof of anything, Sean."

"Maybe not, but immediate response could mean this place is super active," Sean responded, smiling. There was something about feeling vindicated that made everything less spooky. "Okay, if you are trapped here, possibly needing help to get away, please turn on the flashlight to my left."

Several minutes passed with little success. Nothing happened. Neither light changed. His momentary victory seemed light years away. Devon, as always, looked vaguely bored. Sean figured he was probably thinking about smoking a cigarette. Such a terrible habit.

"Alright, that's not a bad thing. If you aren't trapped here, are you choosing to stay? Same response, but if you could turn on the left light, and shut off the right, I will take that as a solid answer."

They waited, Sean sweating slightly under his hoodie. It wasn't warm in the house, it was actually chilly, but the wait—the eternal search for answers—could build up an anxious sweat like no other.

The right light clicked off.

Come on, come on, come on! Sean thought. He so desperately wanted to be right, to prove to Devon that ghosts were real. To get something at least seemingly conclusive for the channel. That was how you got clicks, got views.

The left light clicked on.

Sean almost gasped, catching himself at the last second. "So, you are choosing to stay even though you could pass on? What kind of feelings could influence a decision like that?" Sean cursed himself, remembering that he only had two flashlights with which they could communicate whatever he asked. "Right, of course—you can only answer yes or no. Is there something in this house that is still keeping you here? If so, please turn off the left ligh—"

Before Sean could finish the word, the left light blinked out of existence. Devon leaned forward, taking a keen interest now.

"If we were to offer to help you recover it, would that help you? Maybe let you move on?" Devon questioned, stepping forward to tap on the left flashlight. "If so, turn the left light back off and turn on the right one."

For a moment nothing happened. Devon, always the least patient of the two, leaned forward. "Again, please turn off the left light, and then turn on the right. Only in that order will I believe you are communicating with us."

Sean internally cursed at Devon's wording. They had been over this before. Sometimes giving a specifically-worded instruction led to nothing at all. Much better to ask for one off and the other on, accepting whatever order it happens. Of course, this was imperfect. It was a set of goddamn flashlights, for god's sake. No need to complicate it more.

The worst part was Sean knew Devon would look at it as proof if the lights did not move in the exact way he indicated.

First the left light went back off. They waited, Sean with bated breath and Devon holding in his laugh. He didn't believe a single thing coming from this entire crackpot investigation anyway, so why not have fun with it.

Then the right flashlight flicked back on.

Sean shifted his weight from left to right, having trouble containing his excitement. "A very specific instruction being followed, Boomer? Now, as we know, the more complex, the harder it is to follow, and we've gotten our answer. I don't know about you, but I think we've got something special here."

"Yeah, whatever little jig you're doing right now, that's real special. Turning off one flashlight and then turning on the other doesn't seem to be all that specific, dude. I'm not sold at all. If that's specific, then it seems we have an awfully stupid ghost here."

The right light shut off as if in answer. Sean and Devon looked to the flashlights as if the spirit could speak to them directly.

The left and right flashlight started flicking on and off in fast succession, always in the order that Devon had specified.

Devon gulped, a sickening feeling creeping into his bowels, his stomach groaning. Now this, *this* was weird. He looked over to Sean who was staring, dumbfounded, as the flashlights flicked on and off, the left and right flashes bouncing off his open eyes like glass orbs reflecting in the chiaroscuro.

The room seemed to drop several degrees, almost cold. Sean's sweat cooled on the side of his face and armpits. If he had been able to think at all, he would have called it out for the channel viewers.

After almost two full minutes of flickering, the flashlights stopped. Sean let out a rush of breath that sounded almost like a cry. "The, um, the cameras must have gotten all of that, right?"

"Oh, yeah. Totally. Both of ours were on the entire time." Devon turned toward the flashlights. "Well, spirit, uh...I mean Mr. or Mrs. Spirit, if you like, I am super sorry for calling you stupid. I don't know what I was thinking, but I'm definitely the stupid one, okay?" Devon gave the flashlights his best disarming smile.

"Yeah, Boomer is my best friend, and I can guarantee that he is a certified idiot."

"Dude," Devon said, giving Sean a look that told him he needed to stop.

"Right, so, if there really is something here in the house, something that we can find and help you with, would you know where to find it? If you do, please turn on just the right flashlight."

The right light flicked on. Sean gave Devon a look that said, "I told you so".

"Is it in this room? Left light this time, please," Devon said.

Nothing.

"Is it on this floor of the house? Left light again."

Nothing.

"How about the attic? Right light."

The right light flicked on and off.

"Are you not sure or something? That wasn't very definite," Sean said.

"How about the basement?"

The left light flicked on and off.

"Okay, so you're not sure about that one either?" Sean asked again.

"I guess we have two places to check out then. We needed to investigate them anyway, right? Wanna split up?" Devon joked.

"This is a ghost investigation; we aren't freaking *Scooby Doo*, dude. No, we are not splitting up," Sean shot back, hoping the reference would get laughs in the comments, as well as imply the scariness of being alone in this mansion.

"Alright, alright. Let's do the basement first," Devon offered as a peace treaty.

"Yeah, sure. Both places sound creepy as hell, might as well get to it."

As they walked to the door, Devon called over his shoulder, "Hey, ghost, if you have the ability to follow, come and be our guide. If not, we've left you a nice recording device again, in case you want to record anymore audio diaries."

The two of them maneuvered through the house as quickly as they could. There wasn't really a reason to rush, but traveling through the entire place with only headlamps was much scarier than standing still in one portion of the house while fulfilling a purpose. Even if the purpose they were fulfilling was creepy in itself, at least it directed their attention to something other than the dark.

As they reached the bottom of the stairs, a cold breeze blew against the back of Sean's neck. The chill sent a shiver down his spine, but he brushed it off. The house *did* have holes everywhere, and it was autumn.

They reached the basement door, Devon grabbing and turning the knob. It opened and he moved onto the first step. As Sean stepped forward to follow, the door ripped from his grasp, snapping shut right in front of his face.

The door slammed into the seat of Devon's pants, sending him ass-over-head tumbling down the stairwell. It wasn't a short trip.

As Devon bottomed out, he stretched his body out on the floor, completely engulfed in darkness. His headlamp had ripped off sometime during his fall. When he pulled his hand away from his eyebrow, his hand felt slick and sticky. He must have cut it on something. Great. Just the thing he needed to tip the night from good to great. Just great. Truly awesome.

In his anger, Devon reached for the pack of cigarettes in his pocket. The pack was nearly destroyed, but he managed to extract a whole cigarette, pressing it between his lips and lighting it. The momentary light from the lighter, as well as the dull light from the cigarette's cherry burning as he inhaled, lit the room. Well, a portion of the room at least. It looked truly cavernous, as if it lined the entirety of the mansion.

The floor beneath him felt like a mix between stone and dirt. The plume in the air from his unsettling the floor added a hint of dust and fust to the taste of his cigarette. It made him cough harder than he thought possible. He flicked the cigarette across the basement in disgust, and it bounced, before coming to a halt against what looked vaguely like the outline of a workbench.

As Devon craned his neck to the side, still prone on the floor, something snuffed the cigarette out. One second it was burning orange and bright and the next it was just...gone. Devon raised himself to his knees, his back cracking in a not-so-pleasant way. He mentally clocked Sean yelling and banging on the basement door above, but his mind was mostly centered on the cigarette going out. Was he not alone down here? Could he have missed something when he checked the house?

No, he didn't think so. So, what the hell had done that to his cigarette?

Devon finally stood, stretching his back from left to right, cracking it more than once. It felt good, but it belied the coming pain.

Taking a deep breath, Devon strode forward, aiming for the workbench in the darkness. As he neared it, he flicked his lighter for what little light it could offer.

What he saw in the flickering light stole the breath from his lungs. He stood there, frozen, unable to move away. Someone...something...grabbed hold of his arm. He stumbled back, falling again, and tried to get away. The grip on his arm was far too tight. He hit the floor, his arm outstretched at an odd angle. Something popped, and he released a guttural scream.

His scream was cut short.

With Sean banging and yelling upstairs, he never even heard it.

Sean had no idea how long had passed. He tried the doorknob again. Still nothing. What the hell was going on? He had screamed himself hoarse. The last thing he had seen before the door slammed shut was Devon getting bumped forward. He had to make sure he was alright.

Was he crying? His fear and worry over Devon culminated in a complete loss of composure. What if he couldn't get down to Devon and he was hurt? There wasn't an exit down there. Would Devon be stuck? And how long would it take for a rescue team to get here if he was seriously hurt...would they be fast enough?

Each thought was simply too much. Sean sank to his knees, momentarily giving in to the tears. After the loss of Sumera—her parents practically waiting with dripping fangs for something to happen, then deciding that Sean and Devon were the cause of her issues—she was forbidden from speaking to them. Her family structure necessitated she follow the orders. What would he do without Devon? He didn't have friends. People always looked down on his family being rich, not to mention he was a little odd. Devon and Sumera had been a gift.

A creak that sounded very much like an opening door made its way down the hallway, drawing Sean's attention. He panned his headlamp up the hall. At first, he saw nothing, but then toward the back, the door to the kitchen swayed on rusty hinges. Back and forth. Open and closed.

It didn't make sense. With Devon downstairs, Sean should be alone. He believed in ghosts, truly, but he had expected some beeps on the REM-Pod, maybe a whisper on the audio recorder; at best maybe a hazy shape on the night vision camera. Not full blown...whatever this was. Taunting? *Assaulting?*

Whatever was happening, this spirit was clearly in need of help. Other than the aim of absolute proof of life after death, this was the main reason why he did this. To help. So he had to keep going.

Sean headed toward the kitchen door on weak and shaking legs. Just because he intended to help didn't mean that his body did. He forged ahead.

As he made it to the opposite side of the hall, the kitchen door stopped moving. A bead of sweat made its way down his neck, soaking into his hood. The closer he got to the door, the colder the hall became. Finally bottoming out entirely, his breath came out in milky clouds. Still, fear sweat from his body. Sean couldn't think of a single time he had ever been so afraid of the unknown. What was on the other side of that door? His blood pumped an arrhythmic cacophony behind his ears, his blood pressure making him teeter on the edge of panic.

Sean lunged forward, slamming his hands into the door and knocking it in. A plume of dust rose into the air at the motion, an allergy-inducing mushroom cloud. He covered his mouth, coughing, and flashed his headlamp into the kitchen's corners.

Nothing. The room was empty. No murderous squatter, no apparition.

Sean bent over, placing his hands on his knees, and heaved calming breaths into his dusty lungs.

Just as he was coming down, his panic and heartrate leveling out, there was another sound from behind. It sounded as if it was coming from the second floor. Another door? *Someone's definitely messing with me.*

Once again, there was nothing for it. Time to buckle up and figure out what the hell was going on in the Old Mayor's Mansion.

"Well, folks watching at home," Sean began, remembering the camera had been rolling this entire time. "What you just watched was me almost having a damn heart attack. There is something really bad going on in this house, and it's up to me to figure it out. Devon is locked in the basement, and I'm worried about him, but I can't get the door open to help. There's something messing with me up here. So, we're going to figure this out. You're all coming with me."

Heading toward the stairs, Sean heard a noise coming from above. It sounded like a creaky floorboard being stepped on over and over.

"Yep, someone is definitely messing with me," Sean said to the future viewers. "Squeaking a floorboard like it's a freaking piano key. I hope you'll all join me in being pissed if this is some prank and not a trapped spirit. But, just to be sure, I'm taking the EMF reader out. Again, I'll quickly give an info dump to distract myself. This piece of equipment reads the electromagnetic field and any changes in it. It measures in both AC and DC currents, AC mostly being caused by man-made things, so we're looking for fluctuations in DC currents." Sean turned it on, the gauge moving up and down as it powered on.

"Alright, so at the moment we're at a pretty normal electromagnetic level, so we'll use this as a baseline. The EMF reader's bar will indicate when there's a spike, and that will be when we know something is going on, something is there." Sean took a long breath through his nose, letting it out slowly from his mouth. The explanation and acting for the camera were the only things anchoring him to the task at hand, his mind still running, still worrying over Devon.

At the top of the stairs, the air became cold again, and the EMF reader had its first spike. Sean flicked his eyes to it momentarily, before raising them again to look over the second floor. The squeaking floorboard came from the opposite side of the stairs, toward the back of the house.

The nearer Sean came to the back, the louder the squeak became, the colder the air became, and the higher the EMF reader spiked. He stepped forward, breath sucking in like a maelstrom.

Out of the corner of his eye, Sean thought he actually *saw* the floorboard moving. All of the breath left his body in a rush, panic radiating from his scalp down to the tips of his toes. He was going to be sick; this was it. His stomach rebelled. If he saw what he thought he saw, that meant the camera must have caught it too, right? *Proof.*

Out of nowhere, the squeaking floorboard stopped. As Sean neared the one he had seen moving, a noise rang out from above. It sounded like a mix between a bird chirping and a bell tolling.

"You hear that, dear viewers? What we have here is no prank. I believe I am being led to something by the trapped spirit. The EMF readings as I got to the floorboard just now were so high, like nothing I've ever seen before. Almost an electric buzz to the air quality. I think I have to continue on to the end."

Sean made sure his camera was pointed down to the floor as he purposely stepped onto the loose board, making it squeak in the same way it had been for several minutes.

Readjusting the camera to face forward, Sean headed around the corner and mounted the first step leading into the attic. He was still sweating, still panicking, still freaking out over Devon, but would it be so wrong to be a little excited about the prospects of catching actual proof? In all probability, Devon was fine, the door was just jammed really bad, and Sean would be able to figure it out after this.

At the top of the stairs, Sean gently pressed the attic door forward, the hinges squealing in protest as they aired their disuse. The attic was the coldest room yet, but as Sean aimed his headlamp to the left, he saw that one of the back windows was entirely smashed. He gulped down his nerves, casting an eye on the EMF reader, which had picked up again.

The attic was gigantic, probably ranging the entirety of the house. Without halls and rooms to break things up, there was nothing to distract from the sheer size of the place. There was a reason the house had been dubbed a mansion, and the attic was a good reminder of this. The floors were covered with such a thick layer of dust that they appeared almost carpeted. Sean noticed that the dust was undisturbed. No footprints; a solid sheet of grey abandonment.

Wondering where the sound had gone, Sean stepped toward the nearest window, peering out into the night. It had started to rain, the clouds shifting in waves of grey and black; the moon completely covered. Stepping away, he realized that most of the windows were missing more glass than they had. Maybe it had just been a bird then? Was Sean really chasing ghosts that weren't there?

Sean carefully walked his way from one corner of the attic to the other, doing his best to avoid falling in the dust. As he reached the opposite side, he heard the noise again, almost a chirping ring. He was again reminded of a bird and a tolling bell mixed together.

What the hell is that?

Swinging his head around, he froze in abject terror. In the corner of the attic, arranged around what looked like old luggage, Sean could make out the pale, ghastly figures of the mayor's family. Some of them looked pleading, others hungry, as if his mere appearance was more than they could have hoped for.

Sean dropped the EMF reader without realizing what he was doing. It bounced silently in the dust. He tried to scramble backward but kept slipping in the heavy soot. His eyes were glued to the apparitions before him, his panic making his heart beat right out of his chest. He backed away until he bumped into something solid in the empty attic.

FOUND FOOTAGE

"THIS IS CEMETERY POLICE Department Officer Kevin Yang. This is my third recorded video in the review of the recovered tapes from the Old Mayor's Mansion off Route 9. Two cameras were recovered from the attic. At first glance, we have what appears to be a deranged or mentally unstable teen staring off into the blackness of an empty attic. Based off his heavy breathing and frantic behavior, he is clearly terrified. The cameras, one filming in night vision, the other not, captured nothing but some old luggage in the corner of the attic. The kid dropped what was later recovered and identified as an EMF reader, an expensive piece of equipment apparently used in 'ghost investigations'." The officer's emphasis around the last two words indicated his disbelief.

"What's interesting here is what happened afterward. From the camera shaking, it can be assumed the teen is backing up, scrambling away from something that we cannot see. He stops, semi-abruptly, and then the camera drops to the floor, the night vision camera catching the kid screaming his head off to high heaven as he's dragged into the dark by the ankles. For the record, his ankles are seen angled slightly above him. That is why the working theory is that he was dragged by someone." The officer stopped to let out an exasperated sigh. "After, oh, I don't know, a hundred viewings of this clip or so, it has been definitively ruled that there is nothing caught on camera behind him. So what was pulling him away, and where is he now?

“Another piece of particular interest is the audio recording captured within one of the bedrooms. After a lengthy period where the audio matches that on the footage of both teens within the room, there are various bangs, dings, creaks, and apparent whispers. The whispers come to a head right before one of the boys, Sean, starts screaming when the other boy is locked in the basement. The whispering is often inaudible, but indisputably some kind of human voices. Of all the hours of recording, the only truly audible statement whispered has been identified as a man saying, ‘sleeping with the driver…’, but it then cuts out again. I am of the personal opinion that this statement may be directly linked to the audio recovered from the Metlan boy’s home that captured an angry voice rambling ‘…and in my house’. But, with that being said, where and to whom that would lead us is rather weak as the home has been on the market for the better part of fifteen years, and it has stood empty for far longer.” The officer paused again, sighing deeply at his lack of understanding. “Nothing is adding up here. And where is the teen from the basement? The equipment recovered leads us to believe he was trapped down there, but we’ve recovered nothing. Nothing at all.”

WHEN ALL I FEEL IS PAIN

My name is Colton Davies, and I've come to these woods to kill myself.

It's been over seven months since losing Penny, and I can't keep it together any longer. The loneliness, the pain, the aching hole that's bludgeoned its way inside of me, it's all grown to be too much. Now it's rearing its head, begging to tear its way free. I imagine it blowing out of my ribcage like an embryonic Xenomorph.

I had heard of the Suicide Forest, a place in Japan known for its concentrated confirmed deaths by suicide. I always thought about how horrible it was that such a thing could happen. That people could actually *feel* that way, feel it was necessary. Now I was planning on doing it myself.

The thing is, I've felt lost all these months. Reeling from a loss I couldn't control. Crumpling like sand beneath the waves in a hungry storm. When all I feel is pain, what is there left to do? The decision...rather than a desperate plea, it felt like coming home. Not only regaining some semblance of control, but it felt *right*.

Penny, my late wife, was the absolute best of us. The best person. She was kind, understanding, the most empathetic soul you'd ever meet. We bumped into each other in college, and I fell unconditionally and irrevocably in love with her. So, after graduation, when she wanted to return home, I didn't even consider saying no. Cemetery was small, nestled between a bunch of other towns in the Hudson Valley, and naturally, I had never heard of it. If it wasn't for the level of crime, some might even call it quaint. But that's where she grew up and Penny never asked for much of anything, so settling back in her hometown was non-negotiable. I was only too happy to oblige.

When we got her diagnosis, I didn't know how to handle it. Was I meant to be the strong one? I could tell she was struggling, was in pain. As her husband, it was my job to take care of her. To make sure she felt loved and supported, that she felt safe. How the hell could I protect her from something malignant growing inside her?

We "caught" it in the late stage, the many doctors we saw claiming there was little they could do. We mortgaged the house, sold whatever we could, even borrowed from friends. It was never enough. I was forced to watch as the love of my life dissolved into herself. Breaking down bit by bit until she could hardly move from our bed. But that had been her wish, to be at home, to stay in the place that made her feel safest. How could I do anything but agree?

Ducking under a low-hanging branch, I try to think of the happy times, of times I actually felt alive. That's what she asked of me, her final night on this earth. "Don't remember me like this. Please. *Please,* don't think of the pain. I want you to only remember the good. I love you."

Tears cut salty streaks down my face as I try my hardest. I remember her eyes, such a small but beautiful part of her. How she always claimed they were dull and brown, but to me they were the world. Brown would never be enough to describe them. They were vibrant and soulful. The way they took me in made me feel seen, safe. The tiniest hint of humor would make them shine like drizzled honey. The first time I saw them in the sun I knew she was the one. They weren't brown, they were fire. The life in them beautiful, playful and engaging, light sparkling across them like the inside of a shining orange. They were mine. And now they're gone.

The world has seemed less colorful since then.

I spent months trying to think of anything other than the fact that she had left this world, the morbid turnings of my thoughts stealing my breath and crushing my essence. But I had given in. In due time, we always do. Everything I loved, everything I held within my hands, was gone. But not just gone, rotting away.

Were her eyes even still there?

So, yeah, I'm not planning on leaving these woods alive.

After everything, I was of course, completely depleted on funds, so a trip to Japan was out of the realm of possibility for me. But as a New Yorker with an enhanced license, Canada wasn't. In my limited knowledge outside of the state I grew up in, I half expected to need to know French to get anywhere, something that was well outside my wheelhouse. It wouldn't have been for my Penny, who was fluent and deserved to see the world, but that was just one more twist of the knife.

I still had to hitchhike the last length of the trip through Ontario, but luckily, I found someone helpful. Not only did he drive me to my destination, swaths of snow-slicked trees passing by in shades of green blurs, but he insisted I take his tent and sleeping bag instead of the "sheet-like deathtrap" I had been carrying as a meager cover story. I was not an outdoorsman, and although drifting off and freezing to death sounded pleasant, it wasn't what I had in mind, so I relented.

I had researched enough to know there were several Aboriginal communities I had to avoid, not that it would be hard in such a gigantic area, and that I had to hike a decent amount to get past common campgrounds. I wanted to be as alone as I felt. And being surrounded by so many spruce trees overhead made it somehow still feel crowded.

Ducking and weaving through downward-hanging branches feels reminiscent of being in Manhattan as a kid, like every step bumps me into someone else.

My breath comes out in heavy, watery whisps of cloud. I've been walking for hours, and although I invite the pains, my journey is close to an end. So is my daylight. I'll start my next adventure of figuring out how a tent works when I make it to the next break in the trees.

As I WRAP THE second half of a protein bar back into its wrapper, I wonder if the tilt in the tent is due to some mishap during construction, or the bellowing wind. As I worry about a possible storm out here, a little voice in the back of my head tells me I should really finish the bar. That's Penny. Or at least, what I've dubbed as Penny. Since losing her, the weight has fallen off like so much excess, my appetite never really recovering. But I know she wouldn't want me to let myself go, so she speaks to me. I can never bring myself to listen, but it's nice to feel as if she's still here.

My eyes have taken to drooping, but never really closing. It makes for a strange sensation where I'm neither asleep nor awake. Call it ethereal, I float. I subsist. I think of Penny.

I lie back into the sleeping bag. It is far superior; I knew that for a fact without having to try mine. For a second, I curse myself for already forgetting the man's name, but the concern flees faster than I would have liked. That's what I'm left with: a weak attention span, forgetfulness, and an ever-wandering mind. I'd curse myself again, but I'm already forgetting.

What must be hours later, I startle awake. The first thing I notice is that I must have actually slept, the walking having taken it out of me. The second thing I notice is just how dark everything has gotten. Like plunging into a deep pool with your eyes shut tight, except instead of pressure, it's unfathomable darkness. The third thing I notice is just how cold winter is here in Canada compared to New York. My exhales feel heavy and damp even in the tent. The fourth thing I notice is the noises. Is that what woke me?

I do that thing where you turn your head to the side, listening hard. As if that can enhance your hearing, years of headphones on school buses already ensuring it can't. What sounds like scraping comes from outside, and if I'm correct, from outside the little clearing I set up camp in.

I wrack my brain for what the hell could be all the way out here. I hope for wildlife—well, as long as it isn't a fucking bear—but my mind is already doing that thing where every possibility equals a killer in the night. I hold my breath as the sound of a zipper makes its way to the tent. I melt into myself, trying to become as small as possible in the fear the zipper lining is about to flap open.

When it becomes apparent it won't, I allow myself an all-too shaky breath. I feel around the tent, trying desperately to think of what could be in the dark. Mixed with fear, the sense of touch is by far the shittiest. It takes me way too many tries, frantic and handsy in the dark to realize I left my backpack outside after grabbing the protein bar.

God, what a stupid thing to do!

The realization brings with it relief. Of course, protein bars don't have much of a smell, but a bag left unattended...that can attract an animal. First, I feel stupid, and then I feel brave. I slip my legs from the sleeping bag noiselessly. Kneeling, I slowly unzip the tent, waiting a second more before popping out with a roar.

I see a flash of antlers, a giant body, and quick movements. It's too dark, and the moonlight only offers the slightest assistance.

"Is that a fucking caribou?" I call out into the night. I bend over, squinting, as I chuckle nervously. The laugh becomes a sob as I realize where I am, what I'm doing, what I intend to do.

An hour or two later, an unsettling feeling creeps back over me as I lie in my normal daze. I hadn't seen my backpack.

Love is a real fickle thing. It's kind, empowering, ensnaring, and yet it's also capable of stealing your breath, shredding your soul, and setting your atoms on fire. And I have that kind of love with Penny.

Had. I had *that kind of love with Penny.*

I need...what? I don't know—to leave. I need to leave. I'm overcome with the feeling before a panic attack that says if you didn't run, right now, you never will. But I'm already as far outside as humanly possible. So, what now?

It was supposed to be me. *It should have been me. It should. Have. Been. Me.*

I stumble out of the tent toward the rock at the center of the clearing. Landing hard on my knees, I splash icy water over my face. Once, twice, the excess running into the sleeve of my sweatshirt before I can wonder how inadvisable that is. The bite of winter air already freezing the collar of my sleeve.

It doesn't matter; it had done its job. The shock of it jars my brain into its more regulated, serotonin-deprived rhythm. At least it wasn't panic.

I take in my surroundings. The clearing looks the way I remember it. The tent is still lilted to one side, and I see no signs of anything invading my space. But no backpack. I push myself to my feet and head toward the ageless spruce trees. I'll work my way around in concentric circles in hopes of finding it. If an animal rummaged through it, who knows how far it could be.

One circle, two circles, three. This is good. I mean, there are no signs of animals, or my backpack, but something to focus my mind on is almost thrilling. No thoughts, just *walk*. Just *search*. The hairs on the back of my neck stand on end, but I'm too hyper-focused to feel it. Or perhaps I'm simply ignoring it. Who would be watching me all the way out here anyway?

There is silence in repetition. There is reprieve in emptiness. Not the kind of emptiness that feels hollow, just blank. I need a blank slate, even for a little while.

The thing about grieving is that it's lonely. Not just the loss of a loved one, but once those that flock to you for support have lost interest—their minds can't possibly stay zeroed in quite like yours—they slowly dissipate too. While you're still stuck in the stages of grief, others have returned to business as usual. I spent so long angry at them, at myself, for not knowing how to communicate. That barrier in conversation only further alienates you, makes you feel *other*.

I pause to take a break to breathe and realize I can't make out my little clearing anymore. How exact were my circles? How long have I been at it, head down and chugging along? I have no idea, and the treeline isn't the best for making out how far the sun has gone down. Can I walk dead-center and return to the tent? Or will the slightest angle lead me right past it?

I suppose I might be forced to slowly drift off into frozen sleep after all.

The idea sounded better and better. Until the first strike of lightning. The thunder that follows is deafening, and not far off. Tilting my head up at the canopy of eternal conifers, I can hardly make out the darkening sky for all the boughs. Still, the unmistakable sound of rain reaches me. Reflexively, I pull up my hood.

Freezing to death while sopping wet is another story. A less pleasant one. I've got to make it back to the damn tent. But after standing still and staring up, I'm afraid I've let myself get turned around. Bark, leaves, pine needles, twigs, everything looks the same. How the hell am I supposed to know where to go?

I feel pretty confident that I hadn't moved much before I looked up, therefore I should be standing in the direction I came from. I just realized I couldn't see the tent anymore, right? I decide to trust that—to trust myself—and pick the angle I think best with only the slightest bit of second guessing.

The storm's a real doozy. Even with all the branches overheard, the rain still sloughs off my hood, blurring my vision with any motion of my head. The rain quickly saturates the ground. If only it had been raining when I started searching this morning. It's to the point where my hiking boots are leaving deep trenches in the muddy underbrush. I would have had a trail to follow back. Instead, I'm holding on to a prayer and a hope.

After what feels like hours of searching, my boot catches a random root, and I literally stumble back into the clearing. My left knee sinks into the mud where it bashes against something sharp. My hands sink into the grit up to the wrists before I lose my balance and face plant. Spluttering and spitting the mud from my mouth, I struggle to breathe as I take in the scene before me.

The tent's no longer lilting to the side and is instead all over the clearing. Strips of fabric, bug mesh, tent poles, and the sleeping bag, are strewn everywhere. The tent isn't so much broken down as it is dissected, the cloth ripped and torn as if by claws.

What had done this?

What the hell *could* have done this?

My mind races as my bowels turn to ice. I think back to the middle of last night, fumbling in the dark and thinking that it was a caribou in the moonlight. I'd seen antlers and heard heavy footfalls, but it wasn't really light enough to know for sure. Had I assumed that because of the area I was in?

My mind speeds through the possibilities. It shouts, "*wendigo wendigo wendigo*" over and over, becoming a fragmented and syncopated mantra that fuels my blood. Truth be told though, I don't even know what the fuck a wendigo is. Aside from horror pop culture, I have no real frame of reference for where my mind is cycling, but no matter how I try, I can't shake the feeling I'm right. Can't explain away the devastation before me. And trust me, I'm trying.

I crawl forward, drawing the edge of the sleeping bag toward me. The mylar lining is showing through deep gouges in the bag; bits of synthetic and down feathers stick out of the holes at random. I run my hand over the bag, looking for what, I'm not sure, but looking all the same. My forefinger catches on the edge of something and snags. I inhale deeply as I reflexively draw my finger back toward my mouth, a fat bead of blood already dripping off. As I suck the end of my finger to stem the flow, I continue to examine the bag. Finally, I pluck what looks like a piece of broken claw from the bag with my free hand.

I am stunned. The end is jagged—uneven bits obviously broken off from a larger whole—yet the piece is still four inches long. All the hair on my body stands on end and I feel freezing panic lance through me.

What the hell could have done this?

Wendigo wendigo wendigo still runs through my mind like a record skipping. Each repetition skyrockets my heart rate. I picture the hand the claw must have come from, the arms, shoulders and neck of the thing, the kind of face that can hold the weight of antlers. What strength it possesses to fling the bits of tent so far.

A sound like the crack of a whip ricochets around the clearing. I can't tell where it comes from, but it sounds more akin to a log snapping than a twig. My body goes rigid.

I try to pan my eyes around, to take in as much of the area as I can without moving. My hood does little to help my peripheral vision. I don't dare move. I have this sneaking suspicion, this gut instinct, that when I do, it'll have to be fast.

Before I can decide what to do, a little voice in the back of my head (Penny) points out the elephant in the forest. If there really is something hunting me, why not just let it succeed? My body's reactions are normal, fight or flight is part of human DNA, but why not give in? If I'm here to die, why not get it over with?

It should have been you, not Penny. Been you. Not Penny. Penny. It must be you, my inner-Penny replies. Again, I picture decay, missing eyes, grown-out nails. Penny and I beside each other at long last.

Is that really the truth of it? I don't know myself well enough to answer. I feel eyes on me from every direction. Still feel the overpowering urge to flee. The clock's still ticking. Losing the fight, I launch myself to my feet. Taking off in a zig-zag pattern, I battle through the mud and pain of my damaged knee. If I can keep my speed up, if I can numb out the pain, I can escape.

It doesn't take long for me to hear the noise of something big moving behind me. If I can't get myself to go any faster, I'm done for.

I give up on the zigzagging and take off like an arrow, beelining through the trees and gritting my teeth as I hop over logs, through bushes, and any obstacle in my way. I faintly register a branch whipping across my face, a line of blood drawing across my cheek as I do my best to ignore the sting. Still, the pain is grounding, reminding me why I'm pushing, not giving up. In a way it strikes me as odd. After so many months of suffering I hardly believe I can still be surprised by it. The fact that there's a form of it that can bring clarity rather than gutting sorrow even more so.

All the while all I see is Penny. Her light, her smile, her beauty. Radiance.

The sound behind me dulls to minute scampering, the rain again at the forefront. Can I really get away?

I think the noises sound like they're coming from the left. I take a chance and breakaway to the right in the hopes it will give me the space I need to hide. When I think I've made it far enough, and my lungs feel like they're burning enough to set my coat ablaze, I slide to a halt. Slipping myself under a rocky overhang, I backpedal until my ass bumps the back wall. I try to make myself smaller. I'm making too much noise, but I can't get the air in fast enough, the rasping breaths amplified by the surrounding rocks.

A sound like chuffing reaches me under the overhang. I ram my hands over my mouth. I watch in horror as a beast stalks in, rain or saliva dribbling off a horrid muzzle. It walks on two legs, but hunches at the waist, as if its top half is weighing down the rest of its body. The left hand ends in claws, six inches or more, save for the one left buried in the sleeping bag. The right hand appears human with long, dirty nails. Its skin is blackened, necrotic, and I almost retch as its smell reaches me. The rest of its face is too high for the overhang, its antlers out of my line of sight. This is real. Not a caribou. A *beast*. It makes another chuffing sound, steam rising from its nose. I see the head tilt left and right, nostrils twitching, and then it creeps past.

Slowly, I allow myself a shaky breath. If I can just hold out here, perhaps in time it will leave. I place pressure on my eye sockets. This is unbelievable.

A small chuckle sneaks past my hands as I shake my head in disbelief. This could only happen to me. They say bad things come in threes, but for me, it seems like it's just a permanent staple. The chuckle turns to a sob in my throat. I'm drenched, alone, and in the middle of nowhere. And worse, I brought all this on myself.

Before I can brace myself, I feel strong fingers work through my hair. I yelp in pain as I'm dragged forward and tossed onto the ground. Blood seeps out in patches where the hair follicles were no match for my weight. I scramble to my knees, but when I look back, the beast is gone. I shakily move in a circle, taking in every inch of the forest to ensure I haven't missed what I'm looking for.

There. Twenty feet in front of me, the beast stands hunched and huffing steam. Bits of my scalp and hair now hang from its human hand, nails bloodied.

I run, scouring the ground for something useful, praying, all the while keeping the beast in my line of sight. It makes for sloppy work, but I can't lose sight of it. As I round the side of the beast, it lumbers to face me. I see in its turn that the ground inclines behind it. I barely wonder why as I slam overtop a dead log.

The beast draws closer.

Anger and fear plow through me. My hands scramble for anything to defend myself with. My right grips a baseball-sized rock, smooth but with weight to it. I hurl it at the beast from my position on my knees. The rock makes contact with the beast's shoulder, but other than a small thud, there's no reaction. I fumble for another rock and try again. My throws are frenetic, awful. I move closer to the trees, edging my way toward supposed safety. It's clear I haven't hurt it, but why isn't it attacking?

My hands find the largest rock yet. Like a pitcher I wind up, raising a leg for good measure. I even step into the throw, risking distance for power. But the rock ricochets off an antler and shoots into the trees with cacophonous echoes. In our closer proximity, my jaw drops. The beast just stands, staring.

Stares with eyes that are both monstrous and familiar. Brown eyes. But not just *brown* eyes. Its face is a nightmarish amalgamation of human and beast. A patchwork of what once was and should never be. Of the sacred and the tainted. Still, it's not wholly unrecognizable.

Tears pour down my face as I stare back.

"I'm sorry," I scream at the beast. "I'm sorry! I'm sorry you deserved the world, but I was content to have it pass us by. To view it from the couch. The truth is I'm a coward. I feared the more of the world you saw the more you'd understand how little of it you needed to see with me. And then—then you got sick, and we couldn't have gone even if we could've afforded it. I didn't know how to handle it. I couldn't handle it. Any of it. I still don't know how. Because I'm a fucking coward."

A sob escapes me, and I crumble, hands catching in the mud. The beast takes a heavy step toward me, and I notice for the first time that the trees thin behind it, the ground rockier. The tilt in the ground isn't just a hill, but the edge of a cliff.

The latest rock in my hand thumps back into the moss as I scream. "I came out here because I have nothing left. I am nothing. And I couldn't continue that way. But the truth is, I'm so fucking scared of dying, I could never have done it. And even though death seems to have followed me here, I'm too much of a coward to let it happen either."

The beast takes another thundering step toward me and bellows. Its shoulders drop like it's building up to charge. I can feel its anger radiating off it like waves of putrefaction.

I hold up muddy hands in placation. "Okay, okay! That isn't honesty either. It's not that I'm afraid to die. I don't really want to. Not wanting to live a life and wanting to die aren't the same thing. I'm just—just so incredibly afraid of living without you here. Without my Penny. You were my world, my reason for living, and suddenly you were gone. It felt like—it feels like I lost the right to that life. I don't know how to fix that, but I can't keep doing this."

Tears blind my vision as I come undone. I fear I'll miss the beast's movement, but through rapid blinks I see it remains still.

"So, as much as I don't know what to do next, I can't keep doing this. I can't keep living this way. Look at me. I'm a mess. I am just so fucking *empty*. I don't know what comes next, but I know I can't carry you with me...not like this. I'm sorry. I'll always love you, Penny, but I have to go."

With all the strength I can summon I launch myself to my feet, taking off at full speed toward my fate. As I make it to the beast, I bend, driving a shoulder up under its armpit and tackling it forward with me, right off the cliff.

In that tackle, that solitary act, I push all my self-loathing, my anger and hate, my thoughts of death and decay and loss, my inner-Penny telling me it was all my fault, and I let go.

My name is Colton Davies, and I want to leave these woods alive.

—

Author's note:

This story is in no way meant to glorify suicide or suicidal thoughts. It was an incredibly hard and somewhat cathartic write for me, and it is a celebration on wanting, and choosing, to live. If you or someone you know is struggling, there is always a way out. Forward. And there is always a good reason to live.

Hotlines:

USA: 1-800-784-8433 OR 988

Australia: 1800-799-338 OR 131114

Canada: 866-246-9224 OR 988

United Kingdom: 0800-689-5652

India: 000 800 1006 614

Mexico: 001 800 514 3716

And there are many more online, as well as tons of resources.

BONUS: OFF WITH THEIR SLEDS

A Detective Williams Christmas Novelette

Warning:

As stated in the introduction, this is a bonus novelette included with the collection. It is a *direct* sequel to the novel *Welcome to Cemetery*, and as such, is filled with **spoilers! The mystery itself can be read as standalone, just be forewarned if you have yet to read the novel. Read at your own risk or save for later and come back after checking out the novel!**

CHRISTMAS EVE-EVE (12/23)

DETECTIVE ABBY WILLIAMS WAS growing to hate the holidays.

It appeared it would be a white Christmas after all, and Williams was trying her hardest not to be bitter. She viewed the new passenger side window of the Cemetery PD's Dodge Challenger. Remembering the events that took placc was like a gut punch, but now she drove it in remembrance, choosing to feel the pain like the twist of a knife.

It had been snowing throughout the morning, the car's torque making the roads more dangerous than they would have been otherwise.

She turned into the driveway behind another squad car. Pumping the breaks, she skidded to a stop in the slush, barely missing their bumper.

Shit. I've gotta drive something else for the rest of winter.

Heading in, she ducked beneath police tape. The number of civilian gawkers was lower than expected, but with the snow, it wasn't that surprising. An officer was keeping them under control while a newsperson asked a continuous stream of questions the officer wouldn't, and honestly couldn't, answer yet.

Inside, Williams shared a smile with acting Chief of Police, Ed Reyes. She'd taken to shortening his title to "AC," which he loathed; therefore, she couldn't stop. Her old partner was looking better, more himself. Since their (only) months-old ordeal, he was completely cigarette-free. An outcome and a positive Williams hoped would stick. At least today he was without his oxygen tank. His weight was, however, still being supported by a heavy wooden cane. When she first saw him carrying it, she cracked jokes about him being the Hispanic Hercule Poirot. He hadn't understood the reference but ensured her the cane would save her life one of these days. She wasn't so sure.

Looking around her friend, the smile dropped from her face. Half concealed by the entryway wall, Williams saw more than enough of the horrific scene that brought them here.

The call had come in from a concerned neighbor. When newspapers began flooding the mailbox, the neighbor realized something might be wrong. At first, they'd just thought them gone for the holidays, but then the faint smell became a true stench.

Williams couldn't believe it wasn't the first thing she'd noticed. Reyes removed a handkerchief from his back pocket, passing it to her. She took it gladly, placing it over her mouth and nose to block out some of the stench. It didn't work well, and Williams was left with the slight trace of coffee on her breath mixing in with the filth of decaying bodies.

The bodies, of which there were three, were all piled together on the floor. Each was bloated and blued with decay, insides liquifying. As Williams forced herself to look each body over thoroughly, there was one thing that was absolutely certain: all three had been brutally decapitated. Their necks were uneven in places, but with the decay it was hard to be sure of more. Still, they appeared to be hacked.

Looking up, Williams took in the bloody writing on the wall:

OFF WITH THEIR SL~~H~~E~~A~~DS

was scribbled across the living room wall in the victims' blood, the crossed-out "~~H~~" and "~~A~~" leaving runny lines of blood down the wall. The "SL" was smushed, as if it came to the killer as an afterthought.

"What the hell are we dealing with here?" Williams asked Reyes as she re-entered the entryway.

"Three victims and a shitty pun?"

Williams arched an eyebrow at the answer, and said, "I meant what do we have so far?"

"Forensics pulled a blood sample that may belong to our perp, but we'll have to wait and see if we get anything from it. There were also some red fibers found on the victims as well as the carpet. They still need to analyze it, but it looked like pieces of a crappy Christmas tree rug or something. Which, you may have noticed, this family doesn't have."

Why do we always get the weirdest shit in Cemetery? Williams thought. Deciding to keep it to herself, she turned to Reyes to ask for next steps when her phone rang.

"It's Williams," she answered, motioning to Reyes it would just be a moment.

On the other end of the line was dispatch. One of the neighbors had apparently called in a witness testimony rather than walking across the street. They didn't want any "fanfare." Dispatch made a point to say they sounded batshit crazy. Williams assured them she'd handle it and hung up.

Williams guessed she had her next steps.

II

Halfway across the road, Williams paused in her tracks as someone yelled, "I heard their family was crossed up with that mad-house business from the early 2000s." Williams turned in the snowy street but was unlikely to pick the voice out of the growing crowd. She could only hope the officer guarding the house was paying better attention.

She turned back as a car skidded past in the slush, the driver honking and gesticulating wildly, the spinning tires missing her booted feet by inches.

Almost get hit by a car, and yet I'm the idiot, Williams complained to herself. She *had* stopped in the middle of the street though.

Safely across, Williams rang the doorbell at 53 Aquarius. She mumbled curses, attempting to brush salty slush from her pantlegs. A parting gift from the abusive drive-by.

When no answer came, she knocked wind-dried knuckles on the door. Before she could announce to the home-dweller that her knocking was bound to draw attention from onlookers, the door squeaked inward.

A squat, elderly woman opened the door. She wore a painfully obvious hairpiece, and her eyes were so sunken in Williams wondered if they could even absorb vitamin D anymore. Her wrinkled skin came off her face in jowls that would make a bulldog proud.

"Can I help you, young lady?"

"Hello, ma'am. My name is Abby Williams. I'm a detective with the CPD." She flashed a badge for posterity before stepping inside with the woman.

The inside of the house was absolutely immaculate, albeit outdated. Not a speck of dust, nor magazine out of place. It was sparsely furnished but looked like a qualified designer had been hired, with its pops of blue-on-white across the space like porcelain.

"I was wondering if I could ask you about your call to dispatch? About the witness statement?" Williams was directed to sit at a circular dining table. A cup of tea was placed before her.

The woman took a seat across from Williams, lowering herself into the chair like her life depended on it. The chair creaked as it took her weight. She slid her teacup and saucer toward herself with a clink.

"My name's Eugena, but most in the neighborhood just call me Mrs. McGurdy. Lost my mister several years back, but I kept the Mrs. He was my one and only, you see." Eugena McGurdy slid a faded photo across the table, stopping inches from Williams' teacup. She gestured to it, urging the detective to look at it.

The photo showed a much younger Eugena. Her hubby was a tall, heavyset man with a dark brown beard. Thick and bushy. He looked like a jolly fellow. They both looked happy. Almost out of frame were the shoulders and head of a very small child, long waves of hair blocking their face.

Williams still had no idea why she was being shown the photo. Loneliness, she figured.

"That's my love, my Gerald. We had an amazing life together, but he—he was sick."

"Thank you for sharing this, and thank you for inviting me in, Mrs. McGurdy. Now, if you could please tell me what you saw?"

Mrs. McGurdy looked uncomfortable. She shifted herself from side to side, her chair creaking in protest. Maybe she just needed to fart?

"Well, I told them when I called...but it was Santa Claus that did it." Mrs. McGurdy didn't laugh, didn't smile, didn't break at all. She was deadpan, serious.

Williams tried her best to keep the crestfallen look from showing on her face, snapping her notebook shut. "I'm sorry, but you're saying you saw a man dressed as Santa Claus do that to the Andersons?"

"No, no, no," she replied. Sipping her tea, a sliver of color rose in her cheeks. "It wasn't a man *dressed* as Santa, it wasn't *a* Santa, it was *Santa Claus*!"

Williams stared at the woman, dumbfounded. *Batshit crazy has nothing on her*. She sipped scalding tea as she realized her mouth hung agape. A slightly burnt tongue was better than replying. Eventually she'd have to, but for now she just drank.

"I told that officer on the phone it was him, true. I'd seen it with my own eyes. Went down the chimney and everything. A big red suit with white fur and beard. Just instead of a bag of toys, he was carrying a big ol' fireman's ax!"

"Ma'am, not only is it not Christmas Eve yet, but Santa's known for giving bad kids coal in their stockings, not murdering their whole family."

"Maybe the Andersons are particularly bad? Woke me up in the dead of night. It—it must have been after 10:30 PM! I heard a heavy crash, then rustling outside. I scrambled to the window fast as I could and I saw it all. I ain't lying. Reindeer and all. I-I'd swear it on my sweet late Gerald. I'll swear it on the Bible. Or on a copy of *'Twas the Night Before Christmas*. Whichever you prefer."

"Sorry, Mrs. McGurdy, but I don't think that'd be admissible in court."

Williams sipped her tea because she didn't know what else to do. She coughed when the dregs caught in her throat.

Sorry Gerald, and sorry Jesus, but I'm not about to debate the existence of Santa Claus with a fucking crazy old lady.

CHRISTMAS EVE (12/24)

As Williams tied up her bedroll from the top of the precinct cot, working hard to get the blankets as tight as possible, Reyes came around the corner. Two steaming coffees in his hands, and a frown on his face.

"Hey, kid, was afraid this is where I'd find you. Still staying here?"

"It just doesn't feel right going home yet. My mother keeps asking me to stay, but I don't like the way I feel when she looks at me. Like I'm the victim. And I can't go to Katherine's anymore, so..." Williams trailed off, breath catching in her throat.

Reyes stepped forward, depositing the coffees on a small table. He placed a hand on Williams' shoulder. "You'll get through this. Nothing's ever stopped you before."

Wiping a tear from her cheek, Williams smiled at her mentor and friend. "I know. It's just still so raw, so real. I haven't had enough time."

"You can always take a room in my house. We work similar hours...we can save on gas with these damn prices. And with this cane in my life, you'll help me avoid getting a Life Alert."

Williams laughed. Reyes always knew what she needed. And this new level of comfort between them solidified what an important figure he was in her life. She took him in standing before her. She still saw the burns across his jaw and neck that he'd sustained taking down the latest ring of criminals. The skin was healing, however slowly, but it was a scar he'd wear for the rest of his life. Police corruption wasn't the half of it—the two of them had unraveled a plot involving illegally harvested blood and organs, all organized by one seriously deranged teacher, Andrea Nowack.

She stepped forward, throwing her arms around him in a powerful hug. She'd never done this before, but she found she didn't care. She needed it, and it was Christmas Eve after all. Reyes accepted the hug, taking her into his arms and squeezing her back. He winced in pain, but hid his face from her, hugging her all the tighter.

Reyes thought of Isabel and Maria, Williams of Katherine, and yet both were there in the moment together all the same.

II

In Reyes' office, they sat discussing what they had on the case so far. Was this a cut and dry murder, an in-and-out act of passion, or a new maniac in Cemetery they'd have to worry about?

So far, they had a family of three decapitated in their living room with a bloody pun scrawled on the wall. No forced entry, only one witness statement, and a possible blood sample. The lack of murder weapon wasn't a point in their favor either.

"What about the sample? Did we get anything back on it?"

Reyes tossed a file folder across the desk toward Williams, the stack of papers making the perfect *smack* sound. He kept the office much the same as Chief Carter had, albeit with more personal items. A large photo of Isabel, Reyes' late daughter, hung on the wall, forever immortalized at such a precious age, and Williams knew of a smaller one of his ex-wife Maria kept in the desk drawer as well. The absence of cigarette burns on the desk's edge was a welcome change.

Williams flipped the profile open, pawing through the information. "Clark Stevenson, believed to be an alias, former recidivist, and mental patient. Picked up more than a few times for aggravated assaults and breaking and entering. Okay so the rap sheet tracks, but this says he's been dead for twenty years?"

"It's the only hit we got. It was a rushed job with the holiday. Possibly mixed with the other blood too, so it could be wrong. But according to that file, and according to the projected time of death of our victims, he'd been dead for twenty years to the day of the attack. Twenty years exact."

"Well, that seems important, Ed, but I don't believe in the living dead. Or as Mrs. McGurdy would have us believe, zombie Santa. So, where does this put us?"

"I'm not really sure, but one step forward's better than none. The report says he died due to illness complications, but it doesn't go into detail. I've put in a request for more files to be pulled. Hopefully it's one with an actual mugshot. And I've asked for the blood to be run again."

III

Williams and Reyes walked their way around the curve of one of Cemetery's twin lakes. They wanted to feel a modicum of Christmas spirit while thinking over what they had so far. She had Reyes' arm tucked in the crook of her own, just in case his cane slipped in the snow. Her stitches, finally removed, still sat at the forefront of her mind. Especially right now, as she tensed her core in anticipation of slipping in the slush. The pain, the pull of them, was gone, but the impact they made remained.

The lakes were frozen over, kids and adults alike playing ice hockey or practicing their skating. The crowds were a mixture of greens and reds, Santa hats and bad sweaters. Energy was high for a white Christmas. Children rode sleds down the lakes' banks at breakneck speeds. They slid across the ice, frequently interrupting the hockey games. These interruptions were taken in stride, everybody in jolly moods.

Then again, it was Christmas Eve. Why would anyone be in a bad mood?

Williams and Reyes shared a look. The words unspoken, but the message clear. The children's sleds reminded them of the bloody message scrawled across the living room wall.

"Now I know that report has him marked as dead, but just think, what if?" Reyes wondered aloud. "He would be in his sixties now. Hair more than likely greying or white. It's possible. We know he was off his rocker, right? What if the guy really thinks he's Santa? Fakes his own death and goes off pretending to be the big man in red?"

"*Facts*, AC, we deal in facts. Remember?"

Reyes smiled as Williams' statement echoed one of his own. "Yeah, you're a prick," he laughed, "but really, what if?"

"God, I don't know, Ed. What if? Some guy that's been publicly dead for twenty years is decapitating hapless families as Santa Claus? That's almost as bad as not having a lead at all."

"Twenty years to the exact day of the attack," Reyes replied. "I just can't shake that."

"Significant, maybe. But why?"

The walkie on Williams' hip burped to life, forcing Reyes to swallow his response. "Go for Williams."

"Williams, the chief with you, over?"

Williams pressed the button, holding the walkie out to Reyes. "I'm here, what is it?"

"We received a call. Figured you'd want to know right away. Another report of a foul smell from a neighbor's place. This time over at 40 Lakeview Drive."

IV

Whipping the cruiser onto Lakeview Drive, Williams released another stream of curses. The tirade hadn't stopped for the entirety of the ride over. Reyes remained silent, allowing her time to express her frustrations. He wasn't happy with what was happening either, but his healing side was smarting, and he was beginning to get a headache.

She pulled behind several cruisers, their lights still oscillating red and blue. Officers were working a perimeter, hanging police tape and scoping out the property. She keyed the engine off, then rounded the car to see if Reyes needed help. He refused her, but with an obvious grimace. He gritted his teeth, pulling hard to get from the passenger seat.

Williams took the refusal in stride, figuring he meant to keep up appearances in front of the others. However, she noticed how heavily he was relying on his cane. When the department had asked him to step up as acting chief, Williams cautioned he wasn't ready, that he needed more time. But the thing with Reyes was that he didn't really know who he was without the job. Didn't know how to handle the loss of his family without distraction. And he felt pulled to answer the call of duty, something that Williams understood full well.

Reyes led them through the snow to the front door; it already stood ajar. There was a single step up to enter. From the outside, it looked like a pretty log cabin, all wood and brown paint, although it clearly needed some loving. As they entered the space, it appeared to be more of a shack than a home. The kitchen, dining, and living rooms all one not-so large area. The only thing that was closed off was the bedroom, the door shut. A circle of blood had bubbled up from under the closed door. It had grown thick, saturating the carpet and clotting.

Williams drew in a deep breath, steeling herself for what she was about to witness. That, and to prepare to hold her breath for an extended period. The stench already permeated from under the door.

Williams did her best to push the door back while maintaining enough distance to keep her boots out of the blood. The scene was similar to the one the day before. But this time there was only a single body lying in the filth. However, they were accompanied by what looked like bloodied balls of fur. Williams turned away as she realized the family pets had met the same fate as their owner.

All three bodies on the carpeted floor were decapitated, crudely, the skin and viscera hacked at horrifying angles. Above the bed the murderer had again scrawled in dripping blood:

OFF WITH THEIR SL~~HEA~~DS

Williams allowed a moment to take the writing in. Turning to Reyes, she said, "look at it this time. All the spacing is identical and still scrunched together. Even though the murderer knew what they wanted to write they decided to do it the same anyway. Why would they do that?"

"To keep with the shitty pun?"

"But why not just write it as 'sleds' like it's intended to be read?"

"Our best lead is a dead mental patient...dressed as Santa Claus. You want me to try to use reason?" Reyes said, his eyebrows peeking into his hairline.

Williams opened her mouth to respond before snapping it shut, he did have a point. Maybe it didn't make sense because it wasn't going to. Not with this case.

"Hey, Chief, you might want to have a look at this," Officer Vega called across the small cabin.

Vega took the initiative—after a hefty stare from Williams—crossing the room so Reyes wouldn't have to. He placed an old, greying polaroid into the chief's hand. The photo itself was nothing special, a group of people standing together, bunny ears and smiles throughout. They looked to be in their twenties or early thirties, with a couple older outliers. Several of the group appeared to be in scrubs, so perhaps they were coworkers as well as friends. As Reyes studied the picture, he realized the importance of it was *who* was in the picture. He handed it to Williams, who had already been looking over his shoulder.

"Is that the Andersons?"

"Yeah, kid, and I'd be willing to bet the poor soul in there is in this photo too."

Williams stared down at the photo again, a large wooden sign showing "Ringmore Asylum" visible.

V

Guiding the Dodge Challenger back toward Main Street, Williams blew out a heavy sigh. It was almost evening on Christmas Eve, and the case was looking like it was filled with nothing but ghosts.

The Ghosts of Christmas Past, Present, and my Future, huh?

"Ringmore Asylum lines up with the blood sample, sure, but what're we talking about here, Ed? Someone that's been legally dead for *twenty* years? Plus, an *Asylum*? In Cemetery?"

"Cemetery's not necessarily known for getting with the times though, is it? Not that you'd remember, but we had missing kids on milk cartons long after Amber Alerts became a thing. We're always catching up." Reyes pressed a series of keys on the cruiser's computer. Waiting for something to load, he pulled his right leg up with his hands, leaning his cane against it. "Ah, here. Looks like it's been renamed 'Cemetery Psychiatric Hospital.' They kept the Ringmore sign, though."

"Why have I never heard of it?" Williams asked, her lips twisted down in a frown. "I feel like I would have driven by it or something at least?"

Reyes clacked away at the keys, making several mistakes and practically smashing the delete button each time he did. "Sweet Christmas, finally. Originally from the sixties, it looks like the name was switched when ownership changed hands. Any guesses?"

"Oh, god...the *fucking* Nowack family?"

"The fucking *Nowack* family." Reyes scratched at his prickly chin. "After the purchase was made, the hospital started catering to only the *rich* and mentally needy. Other than the revamped name and a 'charitable' puff piece on the philanthropic qualities of the family, it seems like the hospital disappeared from the media. How much are we betting it was on purpose?"

"And who has control of it now?" Williams asked. She felt her heart rate rising, ire set off by the mere mention of the Nowack family. How long would their shadow loom over Cemetery? For a long time, the Nowack family name was synonymous with the town they owned the majority of. Richness beyond belief gave way to greed, and when their wealth was finally assumed by their only daughter, she did her best to remain a positive public figure while doing incredible harm. Her misled self-righteousness bled corruption through every facet of the town and beyond.

Anger, and if Williams was honest, fear, flowed through her veins in chilling circuits. Hadn't they done enough already? Taken enough?

"Well, there were certain contingencies in place involving extended family in case anything ever happened, but due to the ongoing investigation, the FBI has seizure of all their assets. At least for the time being. Due to the nature of the place, it's still operational, which is a point in our favor. If they're huge fans of the family though, waving our badges around might not get us what we want."

"So, what's our angle then? You know I'm never above punching someone in the face." Williams laughed, taking a deep breath to slow her racing heart.

Reyes chuckled with a ho ho ho. "Punching a medical professional might actually get us a better reaction than the badges."

VI

In front of the Cemetery Psychiatric Hospital, the outside of the building was blank, save for a decades-old sign that read "Ringmore." Cinderblock-style walls painted brown stood stories above them. It didn't necessarily *not* look like a hospital, but the lack of signage, lighting, and typical motorized glass doors made it seem like it was meant to be inconspicuous.

So…that's why I've no idea what this place is, Williams thought.

Reyes had made a quick call to see if any agents were stationed at the hospital. Luckily there were two, one of which they were ensured would be waiting for them. The badge-waving and face-punching would have to wait for another time.

It was better this way. Easier.

The agent, whose name they weren't given, led them to a back office, where an aging computer was ready to log into the hospital's digitized records. The agent asked if they needed anything else, then after pointing out a sticky note of the monitor, left, leaving the two of them alone. The sticky note had a username and password scrawled in messy handwriting.

"That was somehow less pleasant than I imagined punching someone would be," Williams said.

Reyes took a seat in front of the computer, leaning his cane against the desk. He entered the login information wrong, twice. He cursed before sliding the computer chair out of the way for Williams. "Come on, kid, I can't do this techy stuff."

"Like typing?" Williams felt the heat coming off him in his seething.

"Alright, fine. My side is killing me. The pain's distracting."

Williams rolled another chair in front of the computer, keying the login information while looking Reyes over. "Yeah, I've seen the way you're relying on that cane. I told you it was too soon."

"Can you imagine the shmuck they would have transferred in if I hadn't?"

Williams could, so she said nothing. Just nodded and pulled up the search bar. She tried broader searches of both the year the man from Reyes' file was supposed to have been committed and the year he supposedly died. This led to nothing, not a single record. Crestfallen, she tried "Clark Stevenson" in hopes the records were under patient names.

That too yielded nothing. She cracked her knuckles, opening and closing her fists to stretch her fingers. Were they hidden on purpose, or was she missing something? She let out a long breath, stumped.

Finally, in a last-ditch effort, she typed and waited for it to load.

Williams faintly registered Reyes mouthing a curse as a wealth of information flooded the computer screen. Files, videos, audio recordings, and medical exam notes crowded the screen as more loaded. Flicking through the first few medical exams they saw things like "full mental collapse," "complete break from reality," and "possible paranoid schizophrenic." All things that could validate the case, but there was still the fact of the death certificate to overcome. Why would a hospital fake a patient's death? Would they release him?

The two examined several folders, the information mirroring more of the same language on the patient's mental capacity. He seemed to go through stages of healing, appearing normal, lucid, strong even. Then he'd revert to his troubled self, as if he was trapped within. In some of the later files, the name in the doctor's notes changed. She wondered if this new doctor had aided in the patient's healing or the regressive episodes.

Part of Williams felt bad for speculating it could be a mental patient, especially one that seemed to need genuine help. But insanity was never in short supply in Cemetery, and it was her duty to ensure the safety of others. She had to cross whatever line the clues tread.

Williams scrolled through more folders than she could count, finally stumbling on one filled with interviews. All dated, the very bottom right had a video marked just months before his supposed death. She double-clicked on the patient interview. It opened full screen, black with a spinning dotted circle the only hint the video was loading.

After a prolonged wait, the video began to play:

"Hello again. It's Doctor Hartley." She began to say more but paused as the man before her started mumbling to himself.

He was large, not just heavyset, but almost hulking in height. Yet he sat on the edge of a bed curled in on himself. Mumbling and rocking back and forth. He had a long beard in the beginning stages of turning white. The rocking on the bed made him resemble a child after a particularly bad nightmare.

The doctor cautiously moved forward, speaking softly and trying to soothe the weeping man. As she stepped into the man's space, he jumped from the bed, grabbing her by the throat. He forced her back toward the wall with such force that her toes were all that touched the floor. As she connected with a crunch, two nurses ran into the room. One called to the man, pulling his attention to the left, his head turning. The other stepped close and slid a needle into the meat of his shoulder. His head whipped to her side as his body began to betray him. He tried to step toward the nurse but couldn't manage, then crumbled to the floor.

Doctor Hartley stood massaging her neck, what looked like a purple circle already surfacing on her skin. She coughed, "This isn't going to work. He's becoming unreachable."

The video turned to black. Williams and Reyes looked at each other, knowing the video quality wasn't good enough to see much. Williams rewound it repeatedly. The doctor's features were obstructed by the struggle, as were the patient's. With a final pause she stared into the frozen face of the nurse, the grainy quality making it hard to see her actual features.

Williams pulled the polaroid from the Lakeview house from her coat pocket; the corners bent from the trip across town. The photo was perhaps just as grainy as the paused video, but as she held it up to examine, she saw that the woman furthest left appeared to be the nurse from the video.

"We need to find someone that works here," Williams said, jumping up from the desk chair.

Reyes struggled out of the chair, reaching for his cane to displace his weight. Williams was well ahead of him before he was able to limp forward. She was on a mission, his odds of catching up slim.

Williams called over her shoulder for Reyes but felt the need of discovery pulling her forward. If there was still someone working here from back then, then maybe she could get the names of those in the polaroid.

Rounding a corner, Williams saw a nurses' station. A group of four men and women sat chitchatting behind the desk. They all looked fresh out of nursing school. One had a microwaved meal peeled open before him. It smelled like mashed potatoes and gravy, but as if it'd been microwaved to the point of being burnt.

Williams hoped she looked more put together than she felt, knowing the speed at which she rounded the corner was a little crazed. Sure they were used to a little crazy around here, she approached.

Her cheeks reddened as a look of confusion and annoyance crossed the young nurse's face. How could an age difference of less than a decade feel like such a cultural divide? "I'm Detective Williams. I'm hoping someone can identify the employees from this polaroid?"

The young nurse scoffed as Williams said "polaroid" as if it were some kind of foreign curse. She looked to be in her early twenties, her personality of the ditsy variety. "You mean like an Instax?" she said.

The nurse who'd been trying to revive his burnt dinner jumped up from his chair. He reached for the polaroid with an apologetic turn to his lips. "Sorry, she doesn't really know what something is unless she sees it on Instagram. Sure, we can take a look."

He stared down at the photo before passing it around. A few of them looked longer than others, but with no signs of recognition. He held the polaroid out for Williams to take back. “No, sorry. None of us have been here long enough.”

“Is Doctor Hartley still employed here?”

“Doctor Hartley has been retired for over ten years,” a genial voice said from behind Williams.

As she turned to see who had answered her—a short, stocky man in a white lab coat—she saw Reyes round the corner.

The doctor stepped forward, hand extended. A badge attached to his lapel labeled him as Doctor Sawyer. Williams shook his hand, taking the man in. He was certainly older than the nurses. A fair amount of grey appeared in his stubble and sideburns, but not so old as to be part of the generation in the polaroid.

Doctor Sawyer nodded toward the polaroid. Williams realized she’d been staring and blinked. He observed the polaroid with a higher level of care than the nurses.

“We’re investigating a crime. We found a blood sample linked to a patient that was here some years ago—”

“And you believe what? That they may be targeting the people in this photo?”

“We aren’t at liberty to disclose anything of that nature, but we aren’t ruling anything out.”

As he stepped away from Williams, echoes of “follow me” could be heard as his dress shoes clicked down the hall.

Williams waited for Reyes this time, who had finally caught up. A sheen of sweat covered his face and he appeared both pale and reddened. Williams tucked her arm around his and pulled him after the doctor, assisting in carrying some of his weight. He didn’t resist her.

Halfway down they turned left into a hall filled with numbered rooms on both sides. The doctor stopped midway and slid back the viewscreen of door 96. Williams could just make out what sounded like giggling before Doctor Sawyer snapped it shut.

Curiosity piqued, Williams asked, "Was that the rec room or something?"

"Oh no. Nothing as fun as that. Just checking on a longtime resident, Carl Stratton." Doctor Sawyer called for them to follow, not offering more in explanation.

Remembrance niggled at the back of Williams' mind, but she was focused on getting Reyes moving again so they wouldn't lose the doctor.

Reaching the end of the wing, Doctor Sawyer stood with his left arm out, ensuring the elevator didn't shut without them. Reyes' cane caught in the gap between the elevator, nearly tripping him, but he forced himself to step straight.

Williams noted how much of his weight shifted to her as she tried to straighten up with him. He relaxed, however slightly, as he leaned back against the wall of the rising elevator.

The bell *tinged* as the elevator reached the fourth floor; the trio exited.

"Doctor Hartley retired shortly after the ownership changed hands. Don't get me wrong, she was well on her way out beforehand, but the change in clientele pushed her out even faster." He turned them down a hall lined with photographs, presumably of retirees by the look of them. "These are the past doctors," Doctor Sawyer said, stopping before a framed picture of an elderly woman with a frizzy tangle of white on her head. "This one is Hartley. She was a lovely doctor and incredible caretaker."

Williams turned from the picture to Reyes and back. The white on her head didn't match the rest.

"Oh, *shit*," Williams exclaimed. "Think I'm onto something, but you'll have to trust me. Call it a working theory, so take it with a grain of sand."

"Do you mean a grain of salt?" Reyes smirked, both curious and amused.

“Salt, sand...take it with a freaking fistful of snow for all I care, so long as I’m right.”

“If ifs and buts were candy and nuts, we’d all have a Merry Christmas, Williams.”

Williams was appalled. “I’m leaving you here.”

As day turned to night, snowfall grew heavy. Without the sun to keep the ice at bay, the roads became dangerous, and the crowds slipped back into their homes for hot chocolates and crackling fires, spending family time together as Williams and Reyes searched for a killer.

They shared a meal at the Cemetery Diner. Luckily their usual haunt was 24/7. The diner boasted a full “Christmas Dinner Meal” but they went for their usuals—a greasy burger for Reyes, and eggs with fries for Williams. Nothing like a comfort meal to fuel working a family holiday.

CHRISTMAS DAY (12/25)

It was early Christmas Day. Snow continued to blanket the town. Soon families would awaken to piles of wrapped presents under the tree, new core memories forming. Children would shout with glee and cry their thanks, shredding overpriced paper to reveal PlayStations, toys, even puppies. Parents would film on their phones and act surprised at the little trinkets they received. They'd bake cinnamon rolls or pancakes with berries, ice sugar and gingerbread cookies, then gift them to neighbors and friends. They would be merry.

But would any of them give a second thought to the families with less? Those families found *head*less?

Williams hadn't slept a wink. Even as Reyes walked back into the precinct, she sat at her desk, researching, and waiting for Reyes to unleash her.

He brought her a steaming cup of black coffee, a frown on his lips. "I told you to get some sleep. Oh, and Merry Christmas."

"More like *Christmas Bloody Christmas*, Reyes." His face scrunched in distaste. "*Black Christmas*? *Silent Night, Deadly Night*? *Christmas Evil*—if you prefer the classics? There really is an endless list I can choose from."

Reyes fumbled with his pocket as if reaching for his cigarettes. He no longer had any. He sipped from a piping hot coffee instead, burning his tongue.

Williams realized too late that his distaste had been at her crassness. Hadn't he been the crude one not so long ago? "Sorry. Thanks for the coffee. And Merry Christmas."

Williams had wanted to sleep, had desperately needed it actually. But she had needed to figure out a few things to see if her theory held up.

Her mother had sent a ceaseless barrage of texts since Friday. After Williams' several dances with death not but two months ago, they'd been spending more time together. It was something Williams loved; however, her mother's need to randomly hug her, as tight as humanly possible—as if the physical action were the only way to ensure her daughter's tangibility—felt like the reassurance a clingy significant other would need. She understood, it was just a lot.

Williams stood, texting her mother back with one hand and reaching for her coffee with the other. "Can we go now?"

II

Williams knocked on the door of 53 Aquarius Street. She had parked the Ford Explorer up the road, forcing Reyes to trudge through a foot of snow as she knocked on each door, asking the same question every time. She already had the confirmation she needed; she was just curious if the neighbors knew.

While she had filled Reyes in on her conversation with Mrs. McGurdy, since he hadn't been present, the finer points of conversation had been missed. He had Williams' take on the woman, as well as her perception, but would his own theory have matched hers? And while Reyes had a beer and went to sleep for a few hours, Williams had left him in the dark for the most part. He trusted her implicitly, he just hoped her theory panned out, and soon. Christmas or not, the chief of police wasn't exactly supposed to make house calls. He was no longer her partner, and while she did need a new one, it would only fly for so long before the questions began. He hoped she was about to cut through the chaff.

Williams knocked again, her hand so dry from the cold that a small crack had appeared between the knuckles. She heard shuffling inside and stepped back. She didn't expect things to go sideways, not with an old, retired lady, but the chances were never zero.

She wasn't the one Williams was worried about anyway.

The door opened a few inches, the chain still secured. If possible, the woman's eyes seemed further recessed than two days prior, black bags from lack of sleep puffy beneath. Her frizzy tangle was in rare form, sticking nearly upright. Maybe she'd just put it on?

Williams flashed her badge again, introduced Acting Chief Reyes, and asked if they could come in. After all, this was official business. The door shut with a snap, the sound of the chain coming through the thick door. She loosened her Glock 17 in its holster, a move that received a raised eyebrow from Ed. Perhaps keeping him in the dark wasn't such a good idea.

As the door opened, Williams stepped in first, eyes scanning the now-familiar space. It appeared empty, but appearances could be deceiving.

"Oh, he isn't here if that's what you're looking for?"

"So where is he then, Doctor Hartley?"

The old woman tutted, blowing air through her nostrils. She'd softened since her retirement photo. Skin loosened with age and weight, but it was undeniable. She didn't try to. There was intelligence there, steadiness. It dawned on Williama that their previous meeting had been an act.

Doctor Hartley grabbed cups and saucers from a cabinet, setting the electric kettle to boil. When it whistled, she set tea bags in the cups and poured. "Shall we sit?"

Williams guided her to the chair farthest from the door. Not likely to be a runner, but chances being what they were, she'd rather be safe. Then she placed the tea on the table and sat.

"You know, the cock-and-bull story you fed me had me going," Williams admitted. "See, I have this drive in me, one that I can't switch off. It doesn't allow me to write anything off, even a witness testimony as batshit crazy as yours. Santa Claus exacting revenge? I thought you'd wasted our time, but still, I couldn't let it go." Williams sipped her tea and Reyes eyed her warily. "See, what you didn't know—couldn't have known—was that we found blood at the crime scene. Blood that wasn't from the victims. It matched a file we had but was old enough that we couldn't find a mugshot right away.

"And when each step of our investigating brought us farther from Santa, and somehow back around to you, I had to realign and digest what we had so far. Had to ditch the sugarplums and candy canes for the facts. Because you tried to call in your witness testimony. You told them you wanted anonymity, but with a call to dispatch, of course we had your information. At first, I'll admit, I thought nothing of it. Just a woman getting on in years wanting to be left alone. Not so unheard of, right?

"Then, you waxed poetic about an epic love story. I'd just found out I had a triple homicide on my hands, but I'm not immune to desires of the heart, therefore I listened. You fetched a photo and forced me to gawk at it, which I did. Again, I admit to noticing you didn't mention the child in the photo but not thinking it all that strange at the time. Maybe you just thought it wasn't relevant to the story, fine. Maybe it wasn't even your child.

"You see Doctor Hartley, twenty-year-old files are stored in the basement, they take time to find them all. They shouldn't, but that's Cemetery for you. So we only had the one alias to go by. Fortunately, the file led us to the Ringmore Asylum. But would you believe it, the alias didn't bring up anything in the database. Stumped, I thought we might have found a dead end. Then in a last-ditch effort, I typed in "Gerald McGurdy" into the search bar. You wouldn't believe the kind of things we found and—"

"It led you right to me," Doctor Hartley finished.

Reyes' eyes lit up as things came full circle. He'd really been slowed by how much pain he was in.

"In quite a roundabout way, yes," Williams said. "I thought I recognized you in a video but couldn't be positive. When I finally saw your retirement photo on the wall, things really clicked. As the precinct slowed for the night, I got to work. I found the missing records, including the lost mugshot, fact-checked a few more things with the psychiatric hospital, looked up the name this house was purchased under—as well as the caller-id your call came in with, and lastly, although I couldn't access medical records, I found an old kindergarten graduation photo. You'd be surprised how closely it resembled the photo you showed me."

Williams smiled at the doctor. Her face was pale, and her ring finger clacked against her teacup. She'd been found out, and even now, didn't deny it.

"When you met your future husband, he wasn't quite the man you boast about, was he? I'd say early twenties, in and out of lock up during a time when aliases actually worked. You tried hard to get him on the straight and narrow, didn't you? But I remembered you said that Gerald *was* sick. You didn't say 'got sick' like those who euphemize cancer diagnoses. This was a continuing occurrence, something that didn't go away.

"When he got arrested again, this time for something that would stick, the lawyer pushed to have him treated instead. They sent him away, didn't they? And with a past like his, you'd kept your maiden name. Bought this house, transferring to be with him, but it took time. And that's why your name appeared years into his treatment notes. You gave all your neighbors the name McGurdy, and none of them cared enough to check.

Nothing at home linking to work, and nothing at work linking you to your patient...clever really."

Doctor Hartley's lips twitched into a terse smile. She looked defeated, and Williams briefly felt sorry for her. "And all because of a blood sample..."

"And because you involved yourself, Doctor. If you hadn't called, or even if it had remained anonymous, I wouldn't have known your face."

"So her husband *is* alive?" Reyes blurted.

A single tear carved a streak down the doctor's cheek.

"No, Ed. It was a false positive. Like you said, it was a rushed job. That's what happens when the tech has spiral ham and tinsel on the brain. It was a bit degraded from the quantity of blood in the room too, but that's what it matched. So that's the fact checking I did. Gerald McGurdy died, was cremated on premises, and not even his wife had the kind of power needed to fake that.

"But I digress. Remember the child in the photo, the kindergarten graduate? It got me thinking, Ed. Can a blood sample be misidentified for the parent when it belongs to the child? Yes, it can! If the parents pass on the same blood type, or even a mixed one—say 'A' and 'B' to give the child 'AB' blood, there's enough there for false identification."

"And that's what happened here?" Reyes questioned. He'd done a lot of quick catching up but was still missing a chunk of the facts.

"You want to know what I think, Ed? I think Doctor Hartley is the messed-up one. I'm not suggesting at her age she could have done this, but allowing her son to follow in daddy's footsteps?"

Eugena Hartley stood on shaking legs. "My husband was mistreated from the jump! They knew of his case and thought he faked his illness to get away with it. I stopped that piece of garbage doctor, but I couldn't root out all the nurses. Couldn't get them fired. I argued for years he should be released. It was in all my official statements. The staff messed with his meds, constantly fluctuating them. He—he hardly recognized me.

Then during one of his outbursts, one of the nurses was too heavy handed with the sedative. Gerald, he—he went under, but didn't wake up. And those motherfuckers brushed it under the rug! It's only right my son wants revenge. They stole his remaining years from him. From *us*—"

The doctor broke into uncontrollable sobs.

"Mrs. McGurdy," Williams began, hoping the use of her chosen name would soften her. "Where is your son? Let us put an end to this before more people get hurt...maybe even your son."

III

They left the doctor with Officer Vega. She'd divulged her son's location, but it had taken coaxing.

Reyes had called for backup, but the mother warned he had plans to act, and soon. Nothing the two of them couldn't handle, right?

They made a stealthy approach, nothing but clouds of breath and crunching snow.

Jared McGurdy had bounced around, using various locations in Cemetery to avoid detection. He never stayed with his mother, eliminating the possibility of the neighbors noticing him. Williams had an inkling the mother was the brains behind it, and to be fair, if a slew of things hadn't lined up perfectly, they may not have caught on.

Jared never followed his mother to town, so he entered like a ghost.

Today, Jared was planning his next move from inside the Cemetery Diner. Both the detective and acting chief felt fire brewing at the infiltration of their habitual dinner spot. All the more reason to ensure they cuffed him. Williams wondered if he had scoped the place out, maybe even eating dinner at the same time as them. How else would he have known about the one day of the year the place closed?

The parking lot wrapped around the building. A guardrail separated a larger lot beyond that led to a strip mall, a gap in the center allowing entry from both ways. They crept around the back of the larger lot. Thankfully the plowed snow formed a natural barrier to hide behind. Reyes still struggled to bend, his head just barely below the cover. His cane carved a jagged line through the new snowfall. The closer they got to the split, the more ragged his breathing became.

Williams fought the urge to place a palm over his mouth. She felt for him, but what was the point of stealth if he hacked up a lung? Or collapsed.

As she crouch-stepped her way around the wall of snow, hand on the gun at her hip, it didn't matter.

Jared McGurdy stood on the back steps of the diner, flicking ash off a nearly spent cigarette. As their eyes locked, she ground out a curse. He really was dressed like fucking Santa Claus. A full red-and-white suit, black buckled boots, a hat that ended in a fur ball, and round, rosy cheeks. But this version of Big Red had a nicotine addiction, a badly broken nose, and a bloody ax.

He looked much more Billy Bob Thornton in *Bad Santa* than Tim Allen in *The Santa Clause*. And he certainly wasn't jolly.

Before either of the cops could react, Jared kicked the rolling dumpster from his place atop the stairs and shouted, "GARBAGE DAY!"

With a jerk Williams let go of her Glock 17 to scoot out of its way. It spun past, kicking up slush.

With little warning, Jared swung the ax like a baseball bat, letting go as it reached its zenith. Williams was forced to throw herself behind the dumpster, the ax ricocheting off with a cacophonous clang.

Spitting snow and salt from her mouth, Williams raised herself on sodden elbows. Getting her knees beneath her, she saw Reyes leaning his head out to see where Jared had gone. His snubnosed .38 was raised, his cane tucked tightly in an armpit. Lowering it, he released a plume of breath. Weaponless, Jared must have retreated inside.

Williams sighed. This was not how she thought she'd be spending the holiday.

An idea spawning, she motioned Reyes toward her. With slow steps, they inched the dumpster back toward the diner. It had one bum wheel, and although she knew the safety of it was illusory, it still afforded them cover they would sourly be lacking otherwise. If Santa-Jared had thrown away the ax so easily, what more could he have inside?

She slipped the Glock 17 from its holster, holding her breath as she rounded the dumpster. Her nose wrinkled, "what the fuck is that smell?"

The air was laden with the scent of trash from the recently returned dumpster, and something cloying.

"That's the cook oil from those fries you love so much. Once collected for disposal, it can get pretty rank," Reyes explained.

Her stomach turned. They'd entered the rotten underbelly of the place, seeing something off limits. She never wanted to eat fries again. Still, this was *their* place, were they really going to let Jared McGurdy get away with this?

We are so not about to shoot the place up, Williams thought. Hoped.

Inching their way up the stairs, Williams took the lead. She stepped into a shockingly narrow halfway, sliding her back along the wall as she edged toward the illuminated kitchen beyond. So far, so good—and by good, there was no weapon pointed in her face or the swish of a fur-lined coat.

The kitchen appeared empty. At first, she thought she caught movement, but it was just a frypan swaying on a hook in front of the heating vent. Williams had never seen the diner from this side, but she figured there couldn't be too many other places to hide.

Reyes placed a hand on the back of her shoulder, stopping her. Shuffling closer, he drew in a deep breath. He was sweaty again, and Williams realized he really should be carrying his oxygen tank.

More like shouldn't be in the field at all. If something happened to him now, that would be on her. He should be sitting behind a desk, giving orders and staying safe. God, maybe she really did need a new partner.

Williams motioned for Reyes to take the left before easing the double-action kitchen door open. She headed right, letting go of the door once Reyes' elbow propped it open. But as Reyes stepped away, it swung shut faster than he anticipated, catching his cane between with a crack.

That was all it took. Jared stood, crazy Christmas glee on his face, pumping a shell before firing his shotgun at them. The top of a booth disappeared in splinters.

Williams ducked below a server cart, giving Reyes a shove as she did. With his cane stuck, he tilted back into the door, which flapped on its hinge, spilling him back into the kitchen. At least he'd be out of the way.

Williams counted to twenty, then lunged around the corner. The booth gave way to stained carpeting. Her eyes followed the sight on her Glock as she panned around the room, but Jared was gone. The bell above the door hadn't chimed, so he had to still be inside.

She took full-length strides, keeping the side of a booth against her hip as she looked in between each for Jared. She could only hope her vigilance would keep him from decking the halls with her insides.

As she reached the final booth, she saw a door ajar past the bathrooms. She recalled it said "employees only" on the customer-facing side. Until this moment, she'd never considered where it led. All she could see was another bland hallway, thin with wood paneling that had seen better days.

She popped each bathroom door open, making quick work of clearing the stalls before moving on. She did little to mask her movements now, he had no choice but to go up.

The end of the hall led to a staircase. A Santa hat drooped off the bottom step. There was nowhere else for him to go.

At the top of the stairs, Williams braced herself against a metal door. It was old, and she felt cold air slipping through the crack. It chilled her, but not nearly as much as what she was about to do. Where was that backup?

"Jared, you know this is a dead-end right? Your mother told us where you would be so we could try to resolve this peacefully." Williams drew back the slide of her Glock, ensuring the one in the chamber wasn't jammed. "What do you say, huh, St. Nick?"

Bursting through the door, Williams sighted Jared with her Glock but was too slow. She saw the muzzle flare before the sound hit her across the diner's roof. Buckshot pinged off the metal door. Jared pumped the action again, lining up another shot.

Williams dodged, knees sliding in the ice and snow. She just cleared the HVAC unit as more buckshot ricocheted. In her rush, she'd lost her Glock in the snow. The roof was uncleared, the topcoat powdery. The gun sank several inches, disappearing.

Jared's weight crunched through the bottom layer of snow as he approached, each step bringing him closer to the person who wanted to stop his revenge. So much planning, and so much anger, no way he'd be thwarted now.

Williams searched frantically, hands numb as they desperately fumbled. Where the hell was her gun. Where the fuck was the backup?

Jared neared the end of his approach; Williams heard his gasping breaths. If she couldn't find her gun, or will him to have a change of heart, this was it for her. Her hands burned something awful, refusing to search any longer. She sat back, expecting to look up into the eyes of her attacker at any moment.

Reyes charged through the door with a yell. It was enough to distract Jared, and Williams threw a handful of snow into his eyes. He stumbled, and before he could catch his footing, Reyes tripped him with the butt of his cane.

Jared's shotgun clattered across the top of the HVAC unit before sliding noiselessly off the roof. His boot twisted in the ice, and he slammed onto his back with a groan of pain.

Reyes stood over him, pointing his snubnose at his chest. He tried desperately to catch his breath in the cold air. In between heaves, he read Jared his rights, finishing them with a "Merry Christmas, ya filthy animal."

As Williams clicked the second cuff onto his wrist, they heard sirens in the distance. Their backup, always in the nick of time.

Reyes looked pale, but he was chuckling.

"What could you possibly have to laugh at right now?"

He beamed. "I told you this cane was gonna save your life..."

IV

Williams looked up from her computer. The clock said it hadn't been nearly as long as she felt it had, and yet she was still bleary-eyed. The endless paperwork remained her least favorite part of the job.

It still felt odd to look up and not see Reyes smoking on the other end of the office. She wondered in time who would replace him. The entire situation felt wrong, like maybe she should move her stuff over there. That way, the new guy would never really *replace* Reyes, just take up space at her old desk.

At nearly noon, she figured that was enough for the day. Her mother hadn't stopped texting her, and Williams was pretty sure that if she didn't show up soon, mom was bound to show up at the precinct. She was gladdened by their evolving relationship, but she wasn't ready to be picked up by her mom. That was a kind of teasing she just didn't need.

She sipped her coffee, but it was stone cold. She spit it back into the cup before tossing it into the trashcan. Yep, that's enough. She stood, heading for the chief's office.

Her knuckles rapped against the wood frame. Reyes popped up like he hadn't been dozing behind his computer. He bounced his finger on the "enter" key as if he was finishing up something important, but Williams saw the computer light up from its sleep cycle.

She chuckled. "Just came to say I'm done for the day."

Reyes cleared his throat, voice gruff with sleep. "Yeah—yeah, me too. You wanna come over for a drink? You know, with the holiday and all? Bet I could scrounge up something to eat too."

"Mom's been expecting me since Friday," Williams said. "If I don't get over there soon, she might actually call *us* to report *me* missing."

Reyes smiled, but it was slight. "Right. Of course...well I won't hold you. Merry Xmas then."

Williams smiled back at him but didn't say more. She stepped out of the office, making a show of leaving.

Halfway down the hall, she spun on her heels, heading back. Reyes stared down at the photo of Maria in his lap, crestfallen.

"AC," Williams said, unable to hide her smirk. "You're coming too, you idiot, let's go."

Reyes' smile spread ear to ear. "Merry Christmas, everyone!"

ACKNOWLEDGEMENTS

First, I would like to thank you, the reader. Thank you for giving my writing a chance, and from the bottom of my heart, thank you for reaching the end of the collection! If you have enjoyed this story, please remember that reviews and ratings are the things that keep us going! Whether it's on socials or to friends, or dropped on Goodreads and Amazon, it means a lot.

Big shout out to Esther (@BooksCozy), who has not only championed my work (again), but read this collection in each and every form. Thanks to Brenden Rajah and author E. Reyes (*Devil's Hill* & *Night of the Jack-O'-Lantern*) for sensitivity reading Séance, as I wanted a more diverse town without writing someone I am not coming off in any way inauthentic or offensive. Another huge thanks to anyone that grabbed an ARC, early reviews really mean so much to authors.

A resounding thanks to my family and friends, several of which served as ALPHA and BETA readers or just sounding boards for my ideas. And all of which have been instrumentally encouraging.

Thanks again to my editor Ed Crocker, who does his best to make it seem like I knew what I was doing from the start.

SOME STORY BACKGROUND

Believe it or not, all of these stories began as a list of story titles on my phone. Some of which, if you continue to read below, you will learn came from actual experiences of mine or others. The original list was quite longer than the finished product, but as you are learning, things don't seem to stay dead in Cemetery...

Rigatoni Carl was a simple one. I was the sales manager at a furniture store while living in Rochester. I would get so bored that I would put the word rigatoni into the lyrics of songs that played over our radio all day. I have no idea why, but...boredom. This was also during the *Terrifier* craze, and Art the Clown is definitely inspiration here. If you have read *Welcome to Cemetery*, you will recall that Williams was traumatized by someone trying to get her during a police stakeout that she never should have been a part of...this is her prequel story, told from the kidnapper's perspective.

ChupaBogra is actually the story of an experience I had as a young teen. My friend group really walked through the woods day and night to get places, although that's not unique. We really found a mutilated deer out there. In many ways, I am the pudgy Colin...and I did see something out there that day. Something we thought chased us. I am not really a believer in the supernatural or paranormal, however, to this day, I still don't know what we saw. What we thought we saw, has been fictionalize in this story. Oh, and my friend back then seriously did have his dad's gun...

Don't Scream, if you haven't picked up on this yet, is my ode to the classic *Scream* opener. Just with the roles reversed. It's my favorite slasher franchise and it's always evolving. If you love it too, you might want to check out *Your Favorite Scary Movie: How the Scream Films Rewrote the Rules of Horror* by Ashley Culins. I received an ARC of it (and the audio is narrated by Roger L. Jackson!!!) and it's an in-depth look at the entire franchise.

Dinner Date was my idea to include a little humor into the collection. To drop heavy hints throughout the story and to see if anyone would have picked up on them by the end. I mean...a wife of Dracula on the date with a guy that looks like he's the vampire—why not?

Can You Turn It Down, originally titled Ghost Rocker, is a ghostly experience from my sister, just heavily altered. The vent shaft runs straight down, and she claimed she heard things all the time...just like in the story. More than one member of my family has said our childhood home is haunted.

Séance is my attempt to tell a story from an angle that is not my typical worldview. To show how Cemetery is made up of all kinds of people, different people making the town what it is. *Welcome to Cemetery* is a pretty diverse cast (at least I think), but Williams, who is white, leads the show...so this was something new for me. And the reference of *Hocus Pocus* is straight from my heart.

Knight of the Living Dead is obviously a play on the famous title, but it also blended a huge part of the Hudson Valley into the story—The Renaissance Faire. Although in my story I said it was in the town of Cemetery itself, our fair here is actually in Tuxedo, NY. I realized while writing it that I guess I always assumed that our fair was *the* RenFaire...but I'm not sure that's true...

Mr. Cody is the story of my actual aunt's house. She always told us Mr. Cody was in the basement, and it always creeped me out. When I had the idea for the story, I asked her about it...she still swears it's true. While housesitting for her, my mother and I really did put the dishes away just for one to smash to pieces on the floor...we did not get stuck in the basement though. I told the actual story, which is quite similar, in Author*ized* Accounts of the paranormal and unexplained for BibliOccult.

BestGhost is my lovechild. My first release done as a sample, and it took me over two years to finally release these stories all together. The story is heavily influenced by Ryan Bergara and Shane Madej in *Buzzfeed Unsolved: Supernatural* and *Ghost Files*. I hope it keeps getting the love (I hope) it deserves. And if readers keep telling me they wish it was longer I just might...

When All I Feel is Pain is the story that came to mind after a bad breakup. When I needed an outlet, this is what came out. I originally wrote it for a submission that wasn't successful, so I reworked it for this collection. I quite like it. As stated above, this story is in no way meant to glorify suicide or suicidal thoughts. It was an incredibly hard and somewhat cathartic write for me, and it is a celebration on wanting, and choosing, to live. If you or someone you know is struggling, there is always a way out. Forward. And there is always a good reason to live.

Off With Their Sleds, the bonus novelette, was an idea I had for a sequel story almost immediately after finishing the first draft of *Welcome to Cemetery*. With such a silly name I knew it would have to be a short, but I really wanted to make a Christmas horror (crime thriller here), so I did it. Before I got into horror, I was super big into Christmas (still am). Gift giving, gift getting, the shared excitement, the nostalgia of it. So when I started getting into horror, I obviously had to tackle every Christmas slasher and horror I could find (and I'm still going). I hope you caught even a sliver of the nods I threw into the story...my favorite being "GARBAGE DAY" which is straight from *Silent Night, Deadly Night Part 2.* Oh, and chronologically, this would technically have happened between the end of *Welcome to Cemetery* and the epilogue!

ABOUT THE AUTHOR

C. J. Daley lives in New York. He is the author of *Welcome to Cemetery*, his full-length crime thriller debut, as well as this full accompanying short story collection. *BestGhost* was his first sampler on the road to release. He enjoys smaller pieces that give hints to his created worlds at large, and he loves blending genres with dark descriptors. He hopes this won't be the last you hear from him, and if you enjoyed, please consider leaving a review on Amazon, BookBub, Goodreads, StoryGraph, Literal Book Club—or share with a friend.

Follow along for more news @CJDsCurrentRead / @CJDaleyWrites on social media

For more goodies to come, sign up for my newsletter

ALSO BY THE AUTHOR

Welcome to Cemetery

BEST GHOST BOOKS

www.ingramcontent.com/pod-product-compliance
Lightning Source LLC
Chambersburg PA
CBHW020936310726
48980CB00007B/798/J

* 9 7 9 8 9 9 2 5 0 8 2 3 9 *